Jo Hird lives and works in Sheffield. Over the past 15 years, she has been through a major transition after the loss of her first husband to cancer. At the age of 38, she began to re-build her life along with her three children. Within two years of her bereavement, she finished a psychology degree, moved house, began a new career, re-married and took on a blended family of teenagers, plus numerous pets. She is passionate about family life and the nurturing of loving relationships and writes in order to support and give hope to others struggling to rebuild a new life after bereavement.

SPIKE

AND

THE BLUE CHAIR

Written by Jo Hird.
Illustrations by Annabelle Yates.

AUSTIN MACAULEY PUBLISHERS™
LONDON * CAMBRIDGE * NEW YORK * SHARJAH

ISBN 9781788488426 (Paperback)
ISBN 9781788488433 (Hardback)
ISBN 9781788488440 (E-Book)

www.austinmacauley.com

First Published (2018)
Austin Macauley Publishers ™ Ltd.
25 Canada Square
Canary Wharf
London
E14 5LQ

Thank you to all of those who encouraged me through the painful process of writing this book.
Thank you to Katie, Cara, Helen, Cath, Elaine and Rod, my friends who read it through and believed in its worth and kept me going.

Thank you to Lauren, who affirmed me as her step-mum; and to Annabelle, my dear niece, who gave so much advice and encouragement and offered me her talents as an illustrator.

Thank you to Gary Wilton and the saints at All Saints Ecclesall Church who allowed me a three-month sabbatical to finish the final draft.

Thank you to Derek, Emma, Sam, Sally, Lauryn and Alex, who supported and encouraged me and allowed me to write their story.

CONTENTS

Chapter One

Spike Comes Home

"For whiskers show a cat (I know it sounds bizarre)

Precisely just how wide and fat their furry bodies are."

The old woman bent down and stroked the side of the large black cat lying on a blanket on the floor. There were four kittens, all snuggling up to her and feeding from her teats.

"You've got four viewings today," the old woman said to the cat. "Although, Peter won't like it, I'm sure."

What she meant was that all of the kittens were being carried away to good homes later that day but Peter, her grandson, was hoping to keep all of them.

Peter had a close relationship with his Nan and often called in on his way home from school, but ever since the kittens had been born, he came every day. His school was on the same street as his Nan's house, so he was allowed to walk there with the understanding that his mother would pick him up later. The small carriage clock on her mantelpiece chimed out, signalling the time of three thirty and the old lady looked out of the window, sure enough Peter was on his way down the path. He was slurping out of a can of fizzy pop with his head bent right back to get the last drops. As he walked into the kitchen, he went straight to see the kittens,

"Oh look," he said, "they are all feeding from her, she's a good mum, isn't she Nan?"

Nan smiled and stroked her beautiful cat.

"She's like a queen bee, all regal and majestic," she said. "But Peter I need to tell you something."

He looked up at her and knew what she was going to say.

"They have all got to go to good homes and today is our last day with them."

Peter was silent, he stroked the mother cat and looked lovingly at the kittens. One was white and two were pure black, and one was black and white. Peter thought he had never seen anything so beautiful in all his life and he was eight years old now.

The telephone rang and Nan went to answer the call, Peter could hear her making arrangements with someone.

"Yes, that's right, we are the last house on the left, just look for the post box outside. They're all here and ready. OK, see you soon, goodbye."

Nan walked into the lounge and picked up the newspaper; she had a passion for the crossword, so Peter knew she would be fully engrossed. He quickly picked up all four kittens and quietly walked upstairs with them. Although he didn't live at his Nan's house, he had his own room there. Reaching the landing, he now hurried into his room and carefully opened the drawer where his Nan had put some socks and pants, should he ever stay over. He dropped the kittens inside the drawer and closed it. Peter had a full bookcase of books in his room at Nan's and he reached for his favourite story. He was beginning to read quite quickly now and he loved to read stories about animals. He became quite engrossed in his book so when the door-bell rang, it startled him. Peter put his book back into the bookcase and climbed up onto his bed so that he could watch through the window. There was a tall blonde lady standing on the door step, she was holding a basket with a metal cage door on the front of it. Peter held his breath.

"Come in, come in," called Nan as she pulled the door open. "They're through here with their mum having a last cuddle, yours was the black and white one, wasn't it?"

Peter crept out onto the landing so he could hear their conversation better.

"PETER!" Nan shouted. "Where are they?"

Nan came to the bottom of the stairs and saw Peter standing there, he was crying.

"Oh Peter, come on now, we have to say goodbye, show me where they are," she said gently as she climbed the stairs to him.

Peter reluctantly opened the drawer and moved his socks and pants to the side, four pairs of eyes blinked in the light and each of them mewed. He picked up the black and white kitten and kissed its head. The kitten clung to him with claws as sharp as needles. Peter carried the little kitten downstairs and gave him to the lady with blonde hair.

"Take good care of him," he said. "Nan says his mum is a queen so that makes him a prince."

The lady with blonde hair smiled and nodded reassuringly.

"Don't worry, I will and I have three children who will make sure he's treated like royalty," she said.

She took the kitten and placed him in her basket, closing the front cage door. Outside, she carefully placed the basket on the back seat of her car and as she got into the car, she could see a little face peering from an upstairs window. She waved but Peter darted back behind the curtain.

....

The lady with blonde hair was mum to three children. She had been searching for a kitten in order to bring some fun and happiness to her home, her husband was very poorly and times were very hard for all of them. She drove home quite quickly but she was careful to slow down around the bends, she didn't want to risk turning the basket over and frighten the poor little kitten. She was hurrying because soon, she would have to fetch the children from their afterschool clubs and she wanted the kitten to be home safe and sound so she could surprise them. As the car drew onto the drive, she checked her watch,

"Good!" she said. "I have half an hour."

She glanced at the front room window where she could see the back of her husband's head, he was in his usual chair. Having heard the car pull up, he raised his hand to acknowledge her arrival back home but he didn't look out. Carefully but quickly, she took the little kitten upstairs and placed the basket down on her bedroom carpet. Taking a deep breath, she sat down beside it and opened the cage door. Almost immediately, the little black and white kitten walked out. The lady with blonde hair picked him up and looked him over.

"You're all spikey," she said. "That's it, that's your name 'Spike', welcome home Spike."

Spike looked back at her, he liked her blonde hair. *That's it*, he thought, *that's your name, you're 'the blonde one'*.

Spike was very curious about the new room, and it didn't take him long to explore every nook and cranny. The blonde one smiled as he sniffed the dust balls under the bed and sneezed, he tried to play with them but they lifted up into the air and he couldn't reach them. Eventually, she looked at her watch again and stood up.

"I'll be back soon Spike but you'll be quite safe in here."

Spike watched her leave the room and close the door. Left to his own devices whilst she collected the children, Spike had another good look round. First of all, he pulled himself onto the bed, digging his claws into the duvet cover. He sniffed the pillows and pushed his paws into them repeatedly, they reminded him of his mother's soft, warm belly and her teats full of milk. Then he walked over the bed cover, leaving tiny imprints with his paws and jumped onto the dressing table. He startled himself as he knocked several small bottles of perfume over and then he played with the necklaces hanging down from a silver tree. His claws got stuck but he managed to free himself when the tree fell over, depositing all of the necklaces on the floor. He jumped down onto the floor and knocked the waste paper basket over; several balls of paper rolled out which Spike boxed round the room with his paws. In the far corner of the room was another door which was slightly ajar, Spike pushed himself through the door discovering a shower and a toilet. He inspected every corner carefully but when he saw the long piece of toilet paper hanging down from its holder, he simply couldn't resist. He reached for it with his claws and pulled, soon he was almost covered with paper which made him very excited. He pounced all over it and pulled it into the bedroom, scattering it around the room. He was having such fun but then he heard the car pull onto the drive.

Spike climbed back onto the bed and jumped onto the bedroom window sill, he could see the blonde one and her three children getting out of the car and it wasn't long before he heard footsteps coming up the stairs and excited chatter.

"Shush," the blonde one said, outside the door, "I need you to be very quiet and then I have a special surprise for you all."

The noise died down and the door opened. Spike was hiding under the bed by this time and so his first encounter with the children was seeing three pairs of eyes peering at him in the darkness. As they spotted him, they shrieked with joy,

"Oh! Mum it's a kitten."

There were two girls and one boy. Amy was the oldest, Dan was in the middle and Claire was the youngest. The blonde one cleared the mess away that Spike had made and let the children fuss over Spike, they all adored him and she smiled to herself. Amy was a bit scared of him but this was due to the fact that she had no socks on and so every time she moved, Spike tried to pounce on her toes. It made her squeal which made Spike even more excited.

"Don't let him bite my toes," she screamed whilst jumping on to her mum and dad's bed.

The boy, Dan, thought Spike was an absolute hero, especially as he made his older sister scream. The youngest girl, Claire, thought her heart might just burst with joy. She had been wishing for a pet every night, she knew a dog would be out of the question as well as a horse, even though she did have riding lessons. She thought she might just be lucky enough to get a hamster, but a kitten was perfect.

Every school day when the children came home, Spike went mad with excitement. He was perfect entertainment for them. The blonde one would get tea ready and all she could hear were shouts of joy and laughter. Spike was really naughty and they loved it. He would climb up the curtains and leap out from under the beds. If the blonde one was sweeping the floor, he would attack the broom and if she was using the vacuum cleaner, he would jump on and hitch a ride. Every morning, Spike would climb into whoever's bed he could, he would bite toes and tickle them with his fur and then he would pop his head out from under the duvet and purr in their faces. The children loved Spike and Spike quickly fell in love with his new home and family too.

The one person who didn't seem interested in him, though, was Dad, he would just sit in his chair and watch the children having fun with Spike. Spike hated being ignored and it made him crave his attention even more. Each day, he would try a new tactic. He would creep under the blue chair and purr as loud as possible. He would jump up onto the window sill beside the chair and sprawl himself out. Both of these tactics were designed to make him look and sound as irresistible as possible. He wanted Dad to reach out and set him on his knee. But nothing worked. The constant rejection bothered Spike, especially as all the time he could sense that Dad was very sad. Cats may appear rather independent and superior and not at all bothered about human anguish, but this is not true.

Cats are very sensitive to the feelings of those they love and chose to be with and Spike although young was no exception. He noticed everything and he studied his family intently. Although he had been welcomed into this new family and although he had been lavished with love, there was a strange atmosphere in the house, a heaviness hanging over them all. It wasn't always obvious but Spike knew it was there and sometimes, it leaked out.

One day, Dan was outside, he loved to kick his football on the drive and practice doing tap ups, he worked hard at it and hated to be beaten by anything. On this particular day, Spike was outside lying in the sun, he could hear the noise of the football being repeatedly kicked up on Dan's boot. After a while, Dan stopped, he opened the back door and called to his Dad,

"Watch me Dad, I can do one hundred tap ups now."

Spike could see that Dan was very close to his Dad, every day when he came home from school, he would take time to sit with him and tell him about his day. He was gentle and caring towards him and he tried hard to make him happy. Eventually, Dad came to the door, he leaned against the door frame and Spike couldn't help but notice how thin his face looked. He smiled wearily at Dan and watched him perform. The first thirty tap ups went well and Dad started counting.

"Forty one, forty two," and Spike watched the ball go up and down.

"Fifty six, fifty seven," Dad was impressed.

"Seventy five, seventy six," Spike hardly dared to breathe.

"Ninety three, ninety four," Dad was smiling.

But then suddenly, Dan lost control of the ball and it rolled down the drive. Dan fell to the ground in such a rage. He beat his fists on the hard floor and screamed at his Dad,

"I CAN DO ONE HUNDRED!"

"Don't be silly Dan," Dad said. "It's only a game and you did really well, you can do more than me."

But Dan was inconsolable and so Dad retreated back into the house. Spike watched him kicking the gate and punching the air, his face was red and wet with tears. Spike leapt up and landed on the top of the gate, he ran along the top with incredible agility and jumped down onto the ground where Dan was sitting.

"I can do one hundred," he said through gritted teeth, "I wanted Dad to see me."

Spike pushed his furry face into Dan's face and wiped the tears with his fur. He pushed his whole body into him and

Dan started to calm down as he stroked Spike. Although this was the first time Spike had seen Dan lose his temper, he wasn't totally shocked by it. Ever since he had first met Dan he had sensed a certain amount of anger and tension in him. It was always just under the surface and it seemed to be linked to his Dad. Dan stroked Spike and picked him up, he carried him inside.

"I wanted Dad to see me," he said.

But Dad was back in his chair, staring out of the window.

....

Dan wasn't always angry, he loved to laugh and have fun, but Spike had noticed that most of his fun was at someone else's expense. He had seen Dan pick up worms or slugs and chase Claire and her friends around the garden. He would hide behind doors and shout as you walked by to make you jump. One day, he did this to his mother and she was so shocked she fell to the floor. It made her really angry. He would hide pretend spiders in Amy's bed or steal things from her bedroom until she got really cross. If he could get a reaction and make someone cross or angry or cry or scream, he was happy. Spike started to wonder if his turn might come soon and sure enough the day came.

Spike was cleaning himself on the blonde one's bed when Dan ran into the room. He was holding one of Claire's favourite soft toys high up above his head, pretending it was flying and Claire was chasing him. The soft toy was a small grey furry cat, Spike had seen it on her bed and he knew she loved to sleep with it. She was giggling as Dan flew it round the room. He was using a silly voice pretending to be the cat

"Am I a bird or am I a plane?" he squealed. "No! I'm super cat."

But then seeing Spike, he dropped the soft toy cat and picked Spike up instead. Holding him high above his head, he shouted,

"Look! Spike is super cat."

Claire laughed even louder at Dan as he zoomed him round the room along the landing and down the stairs. Spike began to feel queasy. He zoomed Spike past Dad in his chair and into the kitchen. The blonde one had been cooking tea but as the phone rang, she moved a pan off the gas ring leaving the flames burning and went to the hall to answer the call. Dan zoomed Spike down near to the flames changing direction at the last minute. Claire saw it first.

"Stop!" she yelled. "Dan, you've hurt his whiskers."

Dan put Spike down and Spike ran under the settee.

"Mum," Claire called, "Dan's hurt Spike's whiskers."

The blonde one put the phone down and came to see what all the fuss was about.

Dan was lying on his belly looking under the settee, Claire was standing on the settee looking down the back.

The blonde one pulled the settee out and reached down for Spike.

Sure enough, all of Spike's whiskers were singed and shrivelled. Dan was horrified and even Dad came to inspect Spike.

"Dan you have to be more careful, cats need their whiskers so they don't get stuck in small spaces," he said.

"How?" asked Claire

"Well," Dad continued, "if their whiskers can fit through a space, they know their bodies can, their whiskers are always the same width as their bodies."

"Will they grow back?" Dan asked anxiously.

"Yes, I expect so," he replied.

"I'm sorry Spike," Dan said. "I didn't mean to hurt you, I'll make sure you don't get stuck while they're growing back."

Everybody fussed over Spike that evening and the story of how Dan had singed Spike's whiskers and how he would need watching in case he got stuck in small spaces was repeated many times.

....

A few days later, Spike heard the blonde one asking Dad if he could fit a cat flap in the kitchen door, this made him feel quite excited as it meant he would be able to come and go as he pleased. So far, he had been let out into the garden but only if someone else was there to keep an eye on him. Spike didn't like this because cats are fiercely independent, but now, he could look forward to roaming as far as he wanted day or night. He had enjoyed being in the small garden, and many times, he had watched the birds up in the trees. From inside the house he had observed their behaviours and sometimes, he would fill with excitement as they landed on the lawn. He could fall into a trance watching them and his whole body would freeze and twitch. He loved the way they moved and flitted about, so now with his new found freedom, he was fully intending to catch one and eat it and he couldn't wait.

His first opportunity came the following weekend, it was early morning and Spike was padding around the garden.

The fence between his garden and the next-door neighbours had a small gap in it and through the hole, he suddenly saw a bird eating some bread on the lawn. Slowly, he crouched to the ground and started to creep towards it, his bottom moved from side to side with excitement, Spike peered through the hole and he saw his chance. Suddenly, he pounced forwards but only his head went through the hole, the rest of his body was stuck. His whiskers were still growing back and he had forgotten how helpful they were to him. As he pulled himself back out of the hole, the bird flew away.

Spike was not deterred though; looking up, he saw a flock of small birds high up in the tree at the back of his garden. He decided to climb up and get one, after all his claws were sharp and he knew he was very agile and clever at climbing. He jumped onto a branch and maneuvered himself up the tree through the leaves and the branches. But as soon as he was near to the birds, they all laughed at him and flew away. Spike looked down at the ground, he was very high up and this time, he really was stuck. There was nothing for it and so he began to meow in the most pathetic way but no-one heard him, no-one came, his family were still sleeping in their beds.

Eventually, the house began to wake up and Spike could hear the blonde one calling his name. Now, he was missing his breakfast. Spike meowed as loud as he could but it was Dan who came out of the house to look for him. He was being true to his word checking that Spike hadn't got stuck anywhere, although he was not expecting to find him stuck up a tree. Dan ran into the garden and following the sound of Spike's cry, he looked up.

"Don't worry Spike, I'm coming to get you!" he shouted.

Without a moment's hesitation, he pulled himself into the tree and climbed up to Spike. He was scratched on both knees but he didn't care or complain. The blonde one came out to see what was happening and saw Dan half way up the tree,

"It's OK Mum, I've found Spike, he's alright," he called.

Steadily and carefully, Dan climbed down with Spike clinging to him. The blonde one and Dad were waiting anxiously as Dan landed safely on the ground with Spike.

"Well done, son," Dad said.

Dan felt like a hero and he smiled.

Spike felt stupid and embarrassed and resolved that once his whiskers had grown back, no living creature would ever make a fool of him again.

....

It was while Spike was waiting for his whiskers to grow back that he spent more time inside than out. This gave him even more time to study his family. He watched the daily routine of the school run and observed that the blonde one did much to keep the home running as smoothly as possible. He watched Dad sitting most of the day in his chair, friends would visit and try to cheer him up. The blonde one was especially dedicated to her husband's well-being. She spent most of her day, while the children were at school, talking and listening to him. She helped him in any way she could and Spike noticed how she tried to keep the atmosphere as positive and light as she could, playing up-lifting music, cooking nice food and holding his hand.

But the sadness was still there and sometimes, Spike would hear her get up in the middle of the night. She would walk quietly down the stairs and sit in the blue chair that was always occupied by Dad. Spike would run and sit on her knee and soak up all her tears as she stroked him. It made him feel like his fur was growing and he wondered how he could help his new family and what was behind the atmosphere of sadness. The one thing he was sure of, though, was that he was never going to abandon them and he was going to do all he could to help them. This was his family now and this was his home.

Chapter Two

The Blue Chair

"It was one of those temptations that attract most any cat

Like corners of high buildings and the inside of a hat."

Spike had given up trying to get Dad's attention but he still cared about him. To show this, he would often lie down on the floor as close to the blue chair as he could and go to sleep. On this particular morning, he had eaten his breakfast and now, he was watching the family get ready to leave for school.

"I'm heading into town when I've dropped the children at school," Spike heard the blonde one telling her husband.

"I won't be long," she said.

They smiled at each other and Spike saw them hold hands briefly before she left. Dad watched the car pull away and waved to them, the house was quiet so he sat in his chair and picked up his book to read. Spike seldom saw Dad leave the house; although, sometimes, the blonde one would take him out in the car, but never for long. He had also noticed that when Dad moved around the house, he was slow, and Spike could hear his slippers scraping along the floor as if he couldn't lift his feet up properly. He wasn't old but he moved like an old man. As Dad sat and read his book, Spike decided to lie as close to him as he could; he was always ready for a nap after his breakfast. As he settled down, he could hear Dad breathing and turning the pages of his book, slowly Spike drifted off to sleep and he started to dream. In his dream, Spike was floating on a huge cushion. There were birds flying all around him and then one big black bird flew down and landed on his back. Spike could feel the weight of this bird pushing down on his fur and it made him jump; as he jumped, he woke up. But Spike could still feel something on his back pushing into his fur, it wasn't a big black bird… it was Dad's hand, he was stroking him. Spike responded quickly, he pushed himself up into the hand and purred repeatedly, he purred so much it made him dribble. Cats sometimes dribble when they are excited; Spike was ecstatic. But it didn't end there, Dad gently lifted Spike up and placed him on his knee.

Immediately, Spike sensed the intense sadness that was coming from Dad, it was like a heavy pressing pain and he desperately wanted to help. In the emptiness of the house, Dad started to talk. He told Spike how sad he was that he would be leaving his family soon and how much he loved everyone. He hated being the source of so much anguish and he wished he could be popular like Spike was. He told Spike how he had always been the joker of the family and he had always played with his children and made everyone laugh. But now, he just felt weak and useless. All the sad things he had bottled up and couldn't possibly tell his family, he now poured out to Spike. Spike's fur absorbed the tears that were flowing down Dad's face and with every drop, he felt himself grow.

"Look after them for me," Dad said.

And Spike stood up high and pushed his head into Dad's face. It was a done deal.

....

Later that week, Spike decided to go on a night time hunt. He was particularly anxious to test his new whiskers now that they were back to full size and so waiting until the house was quiet and everyone was asleep, he pushed through the cat-flap out into the moonlit night. The first thing Spike wanted to do was to establish his territory and that meant only one thing, a lot of weeing.

He had got a full bladder so he was prepared. He walked to the end of the drive and did a little wee against the fence post. He then walked in a circuit for about half a mile. This took him up the road and around the corner. He trotted past the last few houses on the housing estate and reached the main road. It was much quieter at night, so he crossed over into the field on the opposite side quite easily. The field was full of tall grasses and wonderful smells. The raindrops were still hanging onto the blades of grass and as Spike walked through them, his fur became wet. Reaching the other side of the field, he crawled under the hedgerow, this connected Spike with a steep hill on a country lane. He trotted down the hill and round the bend at the bottom. This brought him back onto the housing estate from the other direction. As he walked this circuit, he found lamp posts and fences and tree stumps and bushes all of which he sprayed with his wee. He could smell the scent of other tomcats so it was important for him to cover it up and claim the territory as his own. No one was going to take it from him and as he trotted round, Spike watched for any opportunity to fight or scare other cats away. This became his nightly routine.

Having marked his new territory, Spike set about his next task. He wanted to bring home a gift for his family. With this in mind, he trotted back into the field and ran along the edge of the hedgerow, the moon was so bright that Spike could see clearly. The hedgerow came alive at night and Spike knew if he waited long enough he would find exactly what he was looking for: a mouse. He crouched down as low as possible in the grass amongst the twigs and leaves and listened intently. His ears pricked up as he heard a rustling sound, Spike grew rigid with excitement and suddenly, he pounced. But all he had in his claws was an empty crisp packet. This was not what he had in mind for his family but Spike was not the sort to give up easily. He crouched back down and waited, listening intently. Suddenly, a movement caught Spike's attention. This time, a small field-mouse ran right past him but Spike was so quick. With one swipe of his paw, the mouse was dead. Spike was so elated, this was his first kill and there could be no more fitting present for his family. He carried his trophy home and laid it very carefully in the middle of the kitchen floor. Spike felt quite weary after all this night time activity, so finding a nice warm spot on the settee, he washed his paws and fell asleep.

He woke up as the blonde one walked downstairs,

"Morning Spike," she said on her way into the kitchen to start the breakfast routine.

Spike jumped off the settee and followed her into the kitchen, he was eager to see her reaction to his little present. But as he approached the kitchen door, the blonde one screamed, Spike looked up in alarm to see her hopping around the kitchen.

"Arrgh! Arrgh! It's a dead mouse, stuck between my toes, I trod on a dead mouse, and it's disgusting," the blonde one was most distressed.

The children ran downstairs to see what all the fuss was about.

"That's gross," said Amy.

"Poor little mouse," said Claire.

But Dan was squealing with delight and laughing out loud.

"Well done Spike," he shouted.

But Spike had already darted through the cat-flap and was running down the road as fast as he could. He spent the whole day in the field, the sun was warm and so he made a little bed in the tall grass and slept soundly. *Perhaps I won't bother with presents again,* he thought and he consoled himself with a firm decision to eat anything he hunted and killed in future, rather than sharing it.

When Spike eventually woke up, it was getting dark. He made his way home checking his territory as he went. He hurried along as he was also aware of how hungry he was. Trotting down the hill, he eventually reached the housing estate and headed back up to the house, it was then that he noticed a big blue light flashing outside. He had never seen this before. Cautiously, he made his way up the road and as he got nearer to the house, he could see that the blue flashing light was on top of a big van. Nearing the driveway, Spike could see that Dad was being helped into the van by two men, they were dressed in green uniforms and the blonde one was waving through the window. They both looked so sad. Spike ran up to the cat flap and let himself in, he jumped onto the window sill next to the blonde one and managed to catch a final glimpse of the van as it drove away with Dad inside.

For a whole week, he hardly saw the blonde one, and the children were strangely quiet. He knew something was different but he couldn't quite detect what. There was a funny atmosphere in the house and it was strange to see the blue chair without Dad sitting in it. In light of this, Spike had decided not to venture too far from the family as he wanted to keep his eye on them all. Of course, he would do his nightly routine and check his territory but apart from that, he was at home. This also enabled him to focus his attention on the unoccupied blue chair.

He took full advantage of its emptiness, sleeping on it and spreading himself across it day and night. It had now been seven days since Spike had watched the van with the blue flashing light take Dad away. He had overheard Amy on the phone telling her friend that Dad was in hospital and that her mum was staying with him. Each day, the children went to school as usual but the blonde one's mother was now collecting them and preparing tea for them.

On this particular day, though, no-one had come back from school and now it was getting dark. Spike was completely alone and he started to worry. He jumped onto the empty blue chair and thought about his family, where were they all and what was wrong? He anxiously pushed his paws into blue cushions repeatedly, trying to find some comfort. He stood up and looked over the back of the chair through the front window, wishing his family to return, and as he did, the familiar scene of his home started to fade from view and Spike found himself sitting on the highest corner of a tall building.

The sun was shining and the atmosphere was hot and dusty. Down below, there was a busy street market and lots of noise and as he took the scene in, he began to hear the voice of a market seller calling out above the bustling noises. It was a strange call but somehow Spike felt the words were just for him.

"Now's the time, now's the time, don't miss your chance to fly."

The words seemed to resonate within him and as he listened, two large black wings began to slowly grow out of his back. In an instance, Spike knew that if he could trust the voice and jump, he would be able to fly. He crouched down low as if he were about to pounce upon his prey, his heart was racing. *How could a cat fly*, he thought but as he pushed the doubts away, he suddenly leapt into the air. His tummy lurched and he could see the ground coming towards him fast but as he stretched his new wings out, the wind filled them and he began to soar up and over the market stalls. People were looking up at him, they were cheering and clapping. Spike felt like a hero. He knew something significant was happening to him, he was changing. As he flew up towards the clouds, he felt like a champion and a king. Even the birds couldn't keep up with him. He flew across mountains and he swooped into valleys, he glided over roof tops and he looked down on the green fields beneath him. The wind took his breath away and his fur shook with the sheer speed of his flying. As Spike flew, he was filled with a growing sense of purpose and strength. He was no ordinary cat; he could fly. As he landed back on the tall building, he heard another familiar voice. It was gentle as though it was being carried on the breeze.

"Look after them for me," it said.

Spike looked up to the sky, *it's done deal*, he thought.

....

The week that followed this strange adventure was one of the worst that Spike had known. Across the weekend, people flooded into the house, there were endless cups of tea being made for everyone, as well as sandwiches to feed the steady stream of visitors.

Spike could hardly get into the kitchen to eat his food. All of the visitors had one thing in common they had all known and loved Dad. At times, they laughed as they rehearsed fond memories of the past. But Spike also heard loud sobbing as people hugged each other. Dan was incredibly helpful and accommodating, he answered the door and checked with his mum if it was OK to let people in. He was protecting her from getting over tired. He even made a few cups of tea and washed up. Claire was very quiet and Amy occupied herself with friends and relished her part time job as a waitress. She didn't seem to show much emotion.

A few days later, Spike noticed that the house was full of flowers, they had been arriving all morning. One arrangement particularly caught Spike's eye; it was on the table in the hall and Spike was told off for jumping up to look at it. The flowers had been cut and arranged in such a way as to resemble a crown. The crown had then been set on a pillow also made out of flowers. It was very beautiful and striking and the blonde one touched it lovingly. Spike decided to escape upstairs as members of the extended family arrived, filling the hall and the kitchen and the lounge. They were all dressed in dark suits even the children were dressed smartly, except for Claire. She came downstairs dressed in her track suit bottoms and her baseball cap.

"You can't wear your cap Claire," Amy said gently. "We're going to church."

"Dad bought it for me," she said.

But she was still not allowed to wear it. She cried as she went back upstairs to change and the blonde one looked as though her heart would break, but Dan was irritated with Claire for making such a fuss.

Eventually, everyone was ready and as they left the house, Spike came back down the stairs and jumped up onto the window sill by the blue chair. He watched as three big black cars drew up outside. The blonde one carried the crown of flowers on the pillow and watched as it was placed carefully on top of the coffin which was inside the first car. Then the whole family climbed into the second and third car and they drove slowly and soberly up the road away from the house. When they had disappeared around the corner, Spike sat down on the blue chair and waited. He knew that life would never be the same for any of them when they returned. He had said his own farewell to Dad but now it was their turn.

He curled up on the blue chair and remembered his promise to look after them all. The magic of the chair had infused him with such a sense of purpose that he knew nothing would stand in his way. Whatever it took, he would protect them and help them and as he waited for their return, he wondered if the chair might work its magic on the rest of his family as it had done so on him.

Chapter Three

Rubbish Days

"For cats know what you're thinking, they know just how you feel

They soak up all your sadness and purr with steadfast zeal."

The best thing about cats is that they're not often moody. They wake up and wash themselves and they think about food and hunting birds. If something or someone irritates them, they might hiss or scratch or simply run away. But they are not like people with lots of ups and downs. Spike was no different, he was usually quite happy, although he could get a bit touchy if someone tried to tickle his tummy, he didn't like that at all. The same could not be said for his family, they were finding it very hard emotionally. They were all trying hard to find a new routine and a new way of living ever since Dad had gone. The blonde one was working hard to keep them all together but sometimes, frustrations and emotions boiled over and exploded into the most frightful scenes. Spike had become quite accustomed to being snatched up and taken hostage into Dan or Claire's bedroom. Sometimes, Dan would slam his door with such might Spike feared the house would fall down around them. Arguments would erupt over the smallest of things and tears would flow like a river down Claire's cheeks. Amy tried to help out but she spent most of her time out with her friends. Spike never took sides, he just let himself be carried away and would listen to all of the hurts and complaints.

This was the hardest phase they were going through, everyone missed Dad so much that they were incapable of comforting each other at times. Spike watched as the grief ruthlessly devoured any sense of peace and calm away; it had an insatiable appetite for emptiness and hopelessness. But this was where Spike fulfilled his purpose, for his presence helped to restore peace and calm and brought something of the comfort they all needed.

He knew it wouldn't always be like this for them, they would get through these rubbish days and soon the loneliness and pain would ease. That was his unspoken message and it brought a feeling of hope. Every tear drop that fell into his fur made him grow and the more he grew, the stronger his message became. He wanted to somehow lift his family up over all of the obstacles that lay in their way, it was like learning to fly, and he knew it would take faith and courage as well as a lot of love.

One day, Spike was waiting for the children to come back from school. Amy was at Beauty College now and made her own way home but Dan and Claire would still get a lift from the blonde one. They were both very dependent upon their mum but it often came out in different ways. Dan wanted to somehow dominate her and make sure she was doing everything he demanded. This didn't go down well with the blonde one and she and her son would often fall out. Spike knew Dan was being unreasonable but he also felt his pain. Dan didn't know how to grieve, he just knew he didn't want to lose his mum as well as his dad. But he held on too tightly and overdid it as he did most things. Spike felt this boy had an incredible force within him which made him want to win at all costs. He was never measured about anything, it was all or nothing with Dan. Claire, on the other hand, was gentle and quiet. She never bothered her mum with how she was feeling but kept it hidden away. She wanted to love her mum and make her better and as a result, the blonde one would seek her company out and cherish her every moment with her. Dan didn't like this and so he set out to disrupt the bond between his mother and his sister.

As the car pulled into the drive, Spike was quick to realise that some almighty row was in full blaze. The blonde one was shouting as she got out of the car and then she slammed the door as hard as she could. Spike ran into the hall just as she and the children burst in. The blonde one didn't stop to take off her shoes or coat, she ran up the stairs and threw herself full length across her bed. She was sobbing uncontrollably. Dan and Claire ran up to see her, but Spike raced them to the top of the stairs. The children were aghast at the spectacle of their mother falling apart; despite all they had come through, they had never seen her like this before. Spike jumped up onto the bed and carefully positioned himself on top of the blonde one's back. He was facing the children as they stared from the doorway and he growled softly under his breath.

"What's Spike doing?" said Claire.

"He's squashing Mum to death with his fat body," Dan said, and they both started to giggle.

The blonde one could feel Spike on her back and she knew he was protecting her, she turned and smiled. That was the signal they needed. Dan and Claire jumped onto the bed.

"Sorry Mum," Dan said.

"Yes, sorry for fighting," echoed Claire.

The children stroked Spike and hugged their mum, the crisis was over.

But Spike witnessed many similar scenes. If only he could lead them to the blue chair and let them feel what he had felt that day, he thought, but he wasn't sure what activated the chair's magic, for he had sat in it many times since his first adventure but nothing had happened. The blue chair had been moved into the front upstairs bedroom because the blonde one had decided to re-decorate the lounge and although no-one would ever get rid of Dad's blue chair, it simply didn't fit with the new furniture that had been delivered. The front upstairs bedroom was quite attractive to Spike because it meant he could sleep in the blue chair but also jump easily onto the window sill to keep a lookout for his family returning from a trip out.

Directly after tea, Spike decided to sit at the bottom of the drive, he had discovered a nice spot under the juniper bush. It was quite safe from pushchairs and skate boards and bikes and the general dangers of dogs and children at play. Spike had a very low opinion of dogs. He laughed to himself as he saw them attached to a lead. He felt that they were far too full of their own importance and yet, they were never allowed to roam free. He, on the other hand, could go where he liked when he liked, no-one was ever going to put a lead on him. Occasionally, one of the passing dogs would pick up Spike's scent on the breeze and pull their owners over to the bush to chase Spike, but Spike was far too clever. Even if they had slipped their collar, he would have leapt up into the tree and looked down on them. It was the birds that Spike admired and desired, they were a real puzzle to him. He found their little bodies and the way they flittered about so maddening and enticing, but as of yet, he had never been quick enough to catch one.

From his safe cosy spot under the juniper bush, Spike could also see the front of the house and so as he looked up, he caught sight of Claire in the front upstairs bedroom, she was drawing the curtains. Spike decided to visit her. He pushed through the cat flap and ran up the stairs, as he pushed the door of the front bedroom open, he immediately sensed Claire's mood. She was sitting in the blue chair, holding her dad's coat, crying softly. Spike watched her as she pulled the big, soft coat with all of its padding up to her face. She breathed in deeply as though somehow it would conjure up her dad again. She searched through the pockets, hoping to find something that belonged to him. Spike had seen this coat before. Dad had often fetched it and used it to cover Claire up if she was lying on the settee, watching TV and had got cold.

"Here, have 'Daddy's Big Coat' to keep you warm," he would say.

From then on, it was always referred to as 'Daddy's Big Coat'.

Spike jumped onto the chair and Claire reached for him. Together, they snuggled into the coat and remembered Dad.

"It's my birthday soon Spike," she whispered, "and I wish Dad could have seen me get to double figures."

The tears flowed down her face and Spike nuzzled her. He wished he could do something to make up for her loss. But even he couldn't replace her dad and all that he would have been to her as she grew up. Sitting in the chair with Claire, he realised that Dad would never see her become a teenager or walk her down the aisle, he would never see her netball goals or witness her becoming famous, he would never see her become a mum or teach her to drive a car or frown at what she was wearing.

All she had was his coat, but all she wanted was to feel his big arms around her again. As they sat together, Claire's tears dropped into Spike's fur and he longed to help her.

Suddenly, as though his wish was granted, the familiar scene of the front bedroom started to fade from view and they found themselves standing in a meadow full of tall grasses and buttercups. The sun was warm and there was a gentle breeze; it was a perfect English summer afternoon. Across the meadow, Spike could see a fence and on the other side, there was a narrow country road. It was there that Spike could see a man. He stood beside a big, red motorbike with silver mud guards and fairing. He was wearing a full set of motorbike leathers and holding a motorbike helmet, and as Claire looked up and saw him, he began to wave and beckon to her. Spike watched as she set off at full speed running across the meadow, she climbed over the fence and hugged the man for a long time. Then he handed Claire a spare helmet and she put it on, Spike watched as she climbed onto the back of the bike and they set off. The bike accelerated up the road and round the bend with Claire holding on for dear life. Spike sat down in the grass and the hours ticked by. He knew that this adventure would bring some much needed healing for Claire and so he waited patiently knowing that his job was to escort her back home safely when she returned.

Meanwhile, Claire was enjoying the sensation of speed and she leaned into the bends as the road twisted and turned. She was so happy, she thought her heart would burst. She held onto the man and she felt safe.

Eventually, they pulled into a lay-by where Claire could see an ice cream van. Dismounting from the bike, they walked over to the van and ordered ice cream. Her dad's favourite ice cream had always been chocolate and that's what the man ordered, she had her favourite which was strawberry. As they sat together on the grass, Claire looked at the man's face.

"Why did you leave us?" she asked.

The man smiled at her. "Claire I will never leave you, I'm always here and one day, we will be together forever. Don't just think of the past, look forward to the future, for that's where I am now and nothing will ever change that."

"Can I come again and see you if I need to?" she asked nervously.

"If you need to," he said.

They finished their ice creams and walked back to the bike.

"I'll go steady this time," he said, "don't want you being sick on me again."

Claire laughed, for she knew what he was referring to. They had been on a family cycle ride years ago and because Claire was only little, she had been put in a toddler seat on the back of her dad's bike. All day, she had whined and moaned and no-one could work out why. She was usually such a content child and then she vomited all over Dad's back. She had heard the story many times. The bike started up and Claire loved the sound of its engine, she climbed on and the man took her back to the meadow.

Spike heard the sound of the bike approaching in the distance and he stood up. Claire climbed off the bike and handed the helmet back to the man. They hugged each other again and then she climbed over the fence back into the meadow. As she saw Spike, she ran towards him, she stopped half way and turned to wave to the man again, but he had gone. She ran all the way back to where Spike waited.

"Spike," she puffed, "I've had an amazing day."

She hardly drew breath as she related her story to Spike. The blue chair had done its magic again and Spike was pleased.

Later that night, Spike checked Claire's bedroom; she was sleeping soundly. Spike felt this was her first restful night since Dad had gone and he knew that she would be alright. Her experience of the chair's magic had been quite different to his but then they had needed different things. He wondered if she would need its magic again or not. Knowing she was safely asleep, he left the house feeling quite hopeful.

It was quite late and although the moon was bright, the clouds partially covered it. Every now and then, the clouds moved and revealed the brilliance of its light. These were excellent conditions for hunting, he thought, but first he was going to check his boundary line. More than once, he had had to fight for his territory and he wasn't going to let it be taken away from him. As he sprayed the lamp posts and fence posts with his wee, he thought about his family. He wondered what they would think about him if they could see his night time persona. He was quite different from the sleepy furry cat that everyone dragged around to pet and fuss. At night time, he was a fighter.

Spike quickened his pace and crossed over the road into his field but as he headed down to the hedgerow at the far end, he began to hear the familiar sounds of a cat whining. It was an eerie sound that can make the blood curdle. Spike froze and detected the sound was coming from the lower end of his field next to the hedge. Someone was on his territory. He walked through the grasses towards the noise, which had now stopped. Eventually, he began to see the outline of a large rat, it had its back to Spike, but in front of it was a young tortoiseshell cat. It was frozen in terror. Spike immediately realised that the size of the rat was unusually big but he was incensed at the thought of a rat defeating a cat no matter how young and inexperienced they might be. He decided to act quickly. Lowering himself down in the grass, he suddenly pounced onto the back of the rat taking it by surprise and with his claws fully out, slit the throat in one move. The rat slumped lifeless to the floor and the tortoiseshell cat turned and fled as fast as it could. Spike chased after it and saw it disappearing into a small bungalow across the country lane just the other side of his field. He decided to let it go at that, as it would probably never venture into his territory again after such a near-death experience. He quickly finished checking his boundary and returned home to sleep; *that rat was a giant,* he thought to himself. As he drifted off to sleep, he remembered his own encounter with the blue chair, he was a cat with purpose and just as he was king for his family, he was king of his territory.

....…..

Chapter Four

Amy

"The more that you ignore a cat, the more they cast their spell

For only your affection will make them bid farewell."

Amy was growing up fast and now at seventeen, she was finding her feet in the world. She was at college and she was learning to drive. She had a part time job as a waitress, so now with her own money, she enjoyed making plans with her friends and as a consequence, she spent less and less time at home. She also had a steady stream of boyfriends. Spike watched her come and go but she paid little attention to him. At first, she had tried to pet him and fuss him but just as Spike would relax and enjoy her attention, she would start to blow her nose as loud as a trumpet. It would make him jump and eventually, he would jump down. Once, he heard her complaining to her mother that Spike had made her eyes go red and stream with tears. The final straw came after he had found his way into her bedroom. The door was slightly ajar and as Spike pushed his way in, he found it unoccupied. His curiosity took the better of him, causing him to explore every corner.

Amy's room was orderly and tidy, unlike her sister Claire's who loved surrounding herself with all of her stuff. Amy had a place for everything and everything was in its place. She loved putting things in straight lines and her bed was always made with the cover pulled smooth and straight. The floor was clear of any clutter and her clothes were always put away and folded neatly. Spike had never been allowed in before and he knew it was probably a mistake for the door to have been half open but he could not resist. The sun was streaming in through her window and so after examining the room thoroughly, he jumped onto the smooth shiny duvet cover and snuggled down on Amy's pillow. It was some time before he heard Amy's voice downstairs; he had been licking his fur and enjoying the warmth of the sun on Amy's bed. But now, he instinctively knew that Amy would not be pleased if she found him in her room and so he hopped down and plopped himself on the landing as if he had been there all afternoon. Of course, Amy knew instantly that Spike had been on her bed because he had left a perfect imprint of himself on her cover. The next day, she blamed him for a nasty rash on her face. She was furious about it, Spike could hear the blonde one trying to calm her down.

She gave her a tablet and suggested she put even more foundation on to cover it up.

Spike had noticed that ever since then, her bedroom door was firmly shut, and that's how he felt it was with Amy, like she had shut him out of her life. Spike still kept a watchful eye on her though. She would often meet friends in the village and talk on the street with them until late. Spike had found out where and so he had a special look-out post which he would visit frequently to check up on her. But she never knew he was there.

There were two main things on Amy's mind: passing her driving test and turning eighteen. The blonde one on top of everything else was helping Amy to practice her driving. Spike had noticed that they had a very comfortable relationship, he thought they were very alike in some ways. But he did worry about Amy and her inability to show much emotion about her dad. She was full of energy and zest but Spike sensed she was covering a lot of grief up. *Her friends didn't always help her*, he thought. They were more concerned with themselves and Spike felt she didn't always possess a great judgement of character. Deep down, she was hungry for love and although her mum loved her immensely, it was her father's love that was missing.

Amy was a determined young woman though and she worked hard. She failed her driving test four times and oh the trauma! Spike would hear her telling her mum about it, beating herself up about her failure yet again. But the blonde one would simply say,

"Right! I'm ringing up for a cancellation, you just need to keep going."

The day Amy passed her test, everyone celebrated, but Spike couldn't compete with a car. He realised that he had done all he could to watch over her and now, he had to trust her to make her own decisions and find her own way. He would do what he could when she was home but that was increasingly less.

Amy planned to celebrate her eighteenth birthday with a family meal, followed by a wild night out with her friends. Much of the wider family gathered for dinner and around 10pm, Amy's friends began to arrive. Spike could hear them laughing and getting ready in her bedroom. The blonde one cleared up and said goodbye to the rest of the family, Spike watched as they shouted their farewells and best wishes up the stairs against the sound of loud music and hairdryers. Eventually, Amy and her friends re-appeared and Spike watched her try to walk down the stairs in the highest pair of stiletto heels he had ever seen. Her dress was as tight as a second skin and there wasn't much of it. If he could have given a disapproving look, he certainly would have. Happily, she and her friends jumped into a taxi and disappeared and the house was quiet at last. Spike began to look for the blonde one, they often shared the last quiet hour of the night together. He finally discovered her in the front upstairs bedroom, she was sitting in the blue chair. Spike jumped onto her knee, got himself comfortable and purred softly

"Hello Spike," she said.

But Spike instantly knew she was feeling sad.

"I can't believe Amy is eighteen."

Spike could see that she was holding a picture of her as a baby and another picture when it had been Amy's fifteenth birthday. It was the last one Dad had celebrated with them. Amy was holding a cake with candles and her dad had his arm around her. Amy was smiling but her eyes looked vacant.

Spike could feel the overwhelming sense of loss. It was always on these special days that Dad was most missed, nothing felt normal and everything was broken and fragmented. Often it was during the late evening that the blonde one would sit and shed her tears. She could no longer distract herself with the tasks of the day, now in the quietness, all she could feel was her own painful grief. She let her head fall back against the cushion of the chair and stroked Spike. As they sat together, Spike wondered if he could will the chair to help his beloved mistress as he had for Claire. He closed his eyes and wished it for her and as he opened them, everything familiar disappeared and they were sitting on the top of a sand dune.

The beach stretched out in front of them and as they looked towards the horizon, there seemed to be no separation between the blue of the sea and the blue of the sky. There were big white clouds that looked like a range of snow-covered mountains hanging in the air and the whole scene had a majestic wildness about it, creating a glorious sense of space. The sun was shining but there was also a warm wind blowing. The blonde one turned her face to the sun and closed her eyes, she savoured its warmth and the breeze blew her hair gently off her face. As she did, the sound of laughter began to carry on the wind causing her to turn her attention to the beach. The waves were gently breaking and running along the flat hard sand was a man. He was holding the strings of a kite which was soaring up high and behind him a young boy was trying to keep up. They were laughing and clearly having fun together. Eventually, the man stopped running and carefully transferred the kite strings to the boy, helping him to keep it up in the air. Spike watched the scene as did the blonde one, but she never moved. The boy was about four years old.

As the blonde one watched, she remembered the baby she had lost. It had happened a year before her husband had fallen ill. The pregnancy was unexpected but joyfully embraced. It was when she went for her first scan that she was told the baby inside her was dead. It was so abrupt and clinical. She had to stay in hospital for an operation and she was devastated. She recalled how many evenings she and her husband had cried over that baby; the one they never got to hold in their arms. That was four years ago. But how much harder her life would had been in recent times with a baby to look after as well, she thought. Spike sensed that it was somehow enough for the blonde one to watch this scene rather than to run into it. He could feel the comfort she received that this husband and baby were not completely lost to her, they were somewhere in her future, both very much alive. The blonde one looked up at the kite as it soared in sea breezes, she smiled and she envied its freedom.

"They are both completely free," she whispered into Spike's fur.

The blonde one closed her eyes and let the wind blow through her hair, but it was a kind wind that made her feel alive.

....

Whatever strength the blonde one had received through the magic of the blue chair, it wasn't long before she was needing to draw on it. It was about midnight when the phone rang. The blonde one picked it up and Spike could hear the conversation.

"OK love that's fine just get into a taxi and get home, I'll be waiting for you."

There was a pause.

"Yes, we can talk as much as you need to, see you soon, don't worry."

Fifteen minutes later, the taxi drew up outside and Spike watched Amy tumble out. She paid the fare and walked up the drive, Spike could see she was upset. As soon as she stepped into the house, she fell into her mum's arms and sobbed. As Amy's sobbing subsided, she began to talk.

"Why Mum, why?" she said. "All my friends have dads," she gulped between her sobs.

"Why us?"

The reality of losing her dad had hit her 'full on' as she celebrated her eighteenth birthday. No amount of alcohol had deadened the pain; in fact, it had intensified it. A few weeks earlier, she had split up from her boyfriend or rather he with her and this had left her feeling bereft and empty, so now, she could no longer cover the pain.

"Mum how do you cope without Dad, how do you stand the pain of being left?"

This question revealed that Amy was identifying how painful her father's death must have been for her mother. All through her father's illness and recent death, she had kept an emotional distance. Spike had witnessed her filling her time with as much activity as possible, it was a form of self-preservation, but now, the dam had burst and the tide of emotion was flowing. But her question also revealed a full acknowledgement of how strong she thought her mother had been and still was. The blonde one said very little but she listened intently to her eldest child whilst she held her in her arms as if she were a baby all over again.

Eventually, Amy went upstairs while her mother boiled the kettle, it was now the early hours of the morning but no-one seemed to notice. Spike ran up the stairs and pushed the door of the front bedroom open, he was planning to sleep in one of his favourite spots, the blue chair. As he entered the room, he saw Amy sitting in the chair, she was still crying. Spike jumped up onto the arm of the chair and looked at her. This was his chance, he thought, his chance to lead Amy to the magic of the blue chair. He stepped carefully one paw at a time onto her knee but just as he felt the chair might work its magic, Amy stood up.

"Sorry Spike," she said as she tipped him off her knee on to the ground, his body making an involuntary squeak as his feet hit the carpet.

"I going to talk to Mum again."

Spike jumped back up into the chair and curled up in the warm spot where Amy had been sitting, he wished he could be the one to comfort her but he recognised that as she was growing up, she was beginning to take responsibility for her feelings. *Maybe she doesn't need the magic of the blue chair*, he thought, *maybe she is ready to face reality and move on*. He cleaned his paws and listened to Amy and her mum talking until the sun began to dawn. The bond between them was obvious, not only were they mother and daughter, they were two women standing side by side. Spike would have loved to have led Amy to the magic of the chair that night but his wisdom told him that Amy was going to deal with her grief in a more pragmatic and practical way. *Sometimes, we have to sort things out for ourselves*, he reflected as he pushed his way through the cat flap.

Standing in the cold air of the first light of dawn, he lifted his nose up, he loved the smell of early morning but as he walked around the corner, he could also smell another tomcat.

Cautiously, he headed up the hill past an alleyway, the smell was stronger here; as he passed by, he noticed a number of local tomcats talking together. Spike was never one to socialise with other cats but his curiosity got the better of him on this occasion, he doubled back and approached the feline gathering in order to hear their conversation. What he heard made his blood boil, for all of them were discussing the heroic tortoiseshell cat that had assassinated the giant rat that had been terrorising the neighbourhood. They were praising this tortoiseshell cat for ridding the community of an incredible evil.

Spike did not stop to explain the real version of the story to these gossiping cats, instead, he ran directly to the small bungalow on the country lane. Confidently, he padded up the driveway of the bungalow but stopped short of the back door as an outside light came on, triggered by his presence. He froze for a few moments but all was quiet. As he approached the back door, he could smell cat but nothing was going to stop him; carefully, he pushed his head through the cat flap but the kitchen was empty and quiet. He climbed in and waited; moments later, the tortoiseshell cat walked into the kitchen from the direction of the lounge, he was stretching as though he had been asleep. At first, he looked over towards his bowl, hoping some treats were in it but suddenly, he detected he was not alone. Turning slowly, he came face to face with Spike who was growling softly and preparing to pounce. The owners of the small bungalow awoke to the sound of a furious cat fight taking place inside their kitchen but as they ran down the stairs into the kitchen, all they saw were the remains of fur and a few smatterings of blood… the tortoiseshell cat was licking its wounds and the cat flap was hanging off by its hinges.

The following night, Spike had been given his rightful place as king of the neighbourhood for his heroic act of killing the giant rat and the tortoiseshell cat was never seen in his territory again. *Like Amy*, he thought, *sometimes we have to sort things out for ourselves.*

Chapter Five

New Beginnings

"Now cats are very clever, and they choose whom they will like

They're not easily won over and especially if they're Spike."

Recently, the blonde one had seemed much chirpier, Spike thought. She was still very busy with the children but now, she was turning her attention to the future and she had some important decisions to make. What was she going to do? How would she provide for her children in the coming days? These were serious questions and Spike had heard her talking to her friends about her new plans and ideas. It seemed that she was going to pick up her university degree.

She had started her degree course a year before her husband had been diagnosed but now, she felt it would be a good time to finish it. This was a brave decision, for it meant more change for the family. Nevertheless, she believed it was the right decision. She would not be around as much but she saw no reason why it couldn't work if everyone pulled together. However, the first bone of contention was the fact that the children would have to walk back from school and get their own tea.

"If I'm going to make any kind of life for myself and you kids, I have to do this." Spike heard her telling the children. Amy was fully supportive of her mother's decision as was Claire. But Dan was reluctant.

"I hate walking," he had said as he stomped upstairs and slammed his bedroom door.

The next few months were quite stormy.

Dan was incredibly unhappy about the situation and the only way he knew how to express his unhappiness was through anger. He pushed the blonde one to her limit complaining and goading her into arguments and fights. He yelled at her, punched the wall and refused to co-operate. He would ring her mobile when she was at university and shout down the phone at her if he couldn't find his school bag or his shirt. Everything was her fault and she became the target for his anger. Spike would visit his bedroom often and lie on the bed with him. He would listen to Dan ranting under his breath about how much he hated everything.

He would play on his computer games and if he lost, he would bash the controller against his face.

Spike was constantly alarmed at how self-destructive he was becoming. He knew the blonde one was finding it very difficult as he had heard her talking on the phone to her own mother about it. But time and time again, she would reach out to her son and keep loving and forgiving him. But Dan couldn't get on with anyone in the house and it seemed to fuel his rage all the more if his sisters were being supportive and co-operative with his mother. He would have loved it if everyone was on his side seeing it from his point of view.

One evening, the blonde one was out with her daughters and Dan was home alone. Spike found him sitting in the blue chair in the upstairs front room. Spike jumped onto his knee.

"I hate my life," he said to Spike.

Spike felt his tears fall into his fur, they felt hot like molten metal. Spike was filled with compassion for Dan, he acted so tough and angry but deep down, he was hurting and grieving. Spike began to wish the magic of the blue chair would help him and as he did, everything familiar disappeared and both of them were standing on the deck of a pirate ship which was being violently tossed by the rough seas.

The noise of the wind and the waves and the men was deafening and Spike's first instinct was to find a safe place from which to view the scene. His fur was already wet from the spray as he ran towards the edge of the deck where a pile of rope provided some sense of safety and shelter. Spike looked up and saw two flags blowing in the wind, one was a pirate flag with skull and crossbones, the other had the name of the ship across it. It read 'Furious Rage' and it flapped defiantly against the gusts of salty wind. As the ship tossed and lurched in the stormy seas, Spike dug his claws into the rope and watched Dan. He was dressed like a pirate, holding a sword high in his hand and Spike could see the other pirates gathering around him. Dan began to shout out his orders with a loud voice of authority. Some of the men looked scared and panicky as the waves rose high above the ship but as Dan spoke, they eagerly obeyed him and looked relieved that someone was taking charge.

"Bring the big sail down," Dan cried with confidence. "And you three take hold of the wheel."

He spoke as though managing a storm was all in a day's work for him and everyone did exactly as he said.

Wave after wave tossed the ship around and poor Spike feared he would be sick. But he was constantly distracted from his sea sickness as he watched Dan. All through the storm, he had given orders and seen success and now, the storm was subsiding. As the ship settled down and the seas became calmer, Dan called all of the men to gather around him again. This time, he slowly unravelled a map and laid it on the deck.

"Here's where we are headed and here's where the hidden treasure is supposed to be," he said, pointing at the map.

"If this wind keeps up, we will be there in half an hour; arm yourselves men and get ready to lower the anchor when I give the order."

Dan rolled the map back up and tucked it under his arm and ordered the look-out to let him know the first sighting of land.

The sea was considerably calmer now, much to Spike's relief, but the wind was blowing enough to fill the sails and carry them across the waters to their desired destination. Dan gave the order for sails to be lifted and Spike was amazed at how confidently he took charge of everything. But then as he turned to look across the sea, to his horror, he saw a giant ship bearing down on them. At the same time, the look-out yelled the alarm.

"Ship Ahoy! Approaching from the bow on the starboard."

Dan ran to see the ship with his sword in hand, he was not afraid, he ordered his men into position.

"Battle stations everyone," he shouted, "she's no match for our 'Furious Rage'."

Spike could see the canons ready to fire and the hundreds of men ready to fight. But as the ship came alongside the 'Furious Rage' and the men with swords began to swing across on ropes landing on the deck, Spike couldn't take his eyes off Dan. He sprang into swashbuckling action fighting with immense courage, overcoming the constant barrage of sword and pistol. He ran to give aid to his men where ever he could and saved many of their lives. Down below deck, the pirates rowed with all their might to out run the enemy ship and amidst the canon fire, Dan ordered the men to lift more of the sails as the wind picked up. Eventually, they pulled away from their enemies and as the final foe fell, Dan stood on the top deck with his sword held high above his head.

His men cheered and clapped at his bravery and Dan smiled and savoured his moment of victory. Nothing could beat him and nothing ever would and nothing would take his 'Furious Rage' away.

....

It was about a month after this strange adventure that Spike came back from checking his territory one evening and noticed the shoes beside the kitchen door. He knew everybody's shoes in the house and he had learned to recognise those of regular visitors but these were very unfamiliar. For a start, they were quite big and they were very shiny. Spike could almost see his face in them. He grew strangely suspicious. *Who would polish their shoes to this level unless they were out to impress,* he thought.

He walked into the hall and found the door to the lounge closed, this was unusual. The children were upstairs but he decided to scratch at the lounge door, he didn't like being shut out. It wasn't long before the door opened and that's when Spike saw him. He was tall with dark hair and he looked a little older than the blonde one. He was dressed quite smartly but there was a relaxed feel to him. Spike looked at the man's feet, he was standing in his socks.

"This is Spike, our cat," the blonde one said to him.

"Ey up Spike," he said in his broad Yorkshire accent.

As Spike jumped onto the window sill, they closed the door again. Spike could hardly take in the scene, he felt numb. There were several candles lighting the room and music playing. The Yorkshire bloke was holding the blonde one and softly swaying with her to the music.

Spike watched them together, the Yorkshire bloke gently brushed her hair back from her face and smiled at her. He was incredibly close to her. Spike jumped down and scratched at the door again, he had to leave. He had to find the children.

When Spike was released from the lounge, he ran up the stairs, he found Claire sat in the blue chair, she was holding one of her favourite soft toys. She had hundreds of them all over her bed. Teddies, kittens, dogs, you name it, but she seemed to take great comfort from them. The one she was holding was a little black dog. Spike jumped onto the chair to join her, but she didn't seem upset.

"Hi Spike," she said.

"Eric has a dog," Spike wondered who Eric was, he had not heard this name before.

"He came to watch my netball match last week and he says he's going to teach me how to bowl a cricket ball," she continued.

"He's with Mum now. I think they're in love, Mum says he has a horse as well."

Spike knew this would impress Claire, she had told him many times how much she wanted a dog and a horse, she had written it in red felt-tip on a piece of paper in rhyme and stuck on her wall above her bed, it said:

"Dear God

I know you can do anything

I know you have a plan

So can I have a new Dad and a horse quick as you can

And one more thing I'd love to see

To make it all complete

A dog as well, I'd love a dog to walk along the street"

Spike felt quite concerned about this, he jumped down and wandered along the landing to see Dan. He paused outside his door and sat down, he decided to wash himself as it helped him to think. He laid on his back and stretched his front legs out wide and began to lick all the fur on his belly, stretching his hind leg up, he worked all the way down to his bottom. He wanted his family to be happy and he wanted them to move on, but this was still very difficult. New things can sometimes mean new losses. He had thought he wanted the blonde one to find love again but now it was here he wanted it to go away. He sensed the risk involved. He let himself fall backwards and he moved the back of his head from side to side to scratch himself on the carpet. It was then he remembered the voice of the market seller calling out,

"Now's the time, now's the time, don't miss your chance to fly."

He recalled how it felt to stand on the corner of that high building and to trust the voice enough to jump, if he hadn't jumped, he wouldn't have flown. *Was this the blonde one's chance to fly*, he thought. Nevertheless, he was here to protect his family and if this Eric or Yorkshire bloke, as Spike preferred to call him, was going to become part of his family, he was going to test his motives and see if he was worth his salt. That was his plan and so over the next few weeks, Spike not only observed the love affair, he also put his plans into action.

Claire was obviously on board with this new man but Spike felt she was being mesmerised with horses and dogs, Amy was very supportive to her mother but Spike had already questioned her judgement of character. She was eighteen and a half now but still far too young and what's more, she fell in and out of love every week. *How could she possibly recognise true love,* Spike thought.

The Yorkshire bloke came most evenings now and true to his word, he was teaching Claire to bowl a cricket ball.

He stood at the end of the drive and she would run and bowl at his cricket bat. He would shout encouragement and laugh and joke with her. Claire smiled and laughed a lot too. Spike knew the Yorkshire bloke had also been to every one of her netball matches and they seemed to rub along quite well. Thankfully, Spike had never seen any sightings of a dog. The blonde one seemed quite happy too, she would dress up and wear makeup and obviously enjoyed being wined and dined.

But not everyone was happy with this new chapter unfolding. Dan was plainly hostile and distanced himself, although he was polite if he had to be. Alone in his room, it was a different story. Spike would curl up beside him and hear him rehearsing his anger. Spike sensed Dan's anger flowed from the complete loss of control over his life. Dan didn't want it to be this way but he was powerless to do anything about it. And no matter how hard he fought or how much he shouted his orders, no one seemed to listen and he never felt any sense of victory. The anger was eating him up and Spike was really concerned.

He wished that Dan could trust himself to the uncertain future that was in front of them all. But Dan was a long way from finding his wings and flying. Nevertheless, Spike was determined to help and support him all he could, he just wished that Dan could be happy for those in his family who were beginning to find their wings again.

As the weeks passed and the Yorkshire bloke continued to visit the house, he decided it was time to put him to the test. Spike had three simple tests in mind. Each of them were designed to cause the Yorkshire bloke to react in such a way that everyone would see he was a fake, and that would be that.

He didn't have long to wait to put his plan into action. Later that evening, the Yorkshire bloke arrived and parked himself on the settee. The blonde one was making him a cup of tea in the kitchen and he picked up the newspaper to read it. Spike sprang into action and began to fuss and purr around him, the Yorkshire bloke was pleased to see Spike and responded to his attention, stroking his black velvety fur. It all looked so peaceful but suddenly, Spike lashed out and bit his hand, drawing blood. The Yorkshire bloke drew back surprised and Spike ran out of the room.

"Ow!" He exclaimed. "I think Spike has just marked my card," he said to the blonde one as she brought the tea in. But he didn't retaliate or try to hurt Spike, he was just quite cautious around him after that.

His next test was a little more disgusting. Cats need to cough up fur balls from time to time due to the amount of washing and licking of their own fur. Spike was no exception. He had coughed a rather large, wet one up outside in the garden and hidden it under a bush. He was saving it until the Yorkshire bloke arrived. Phase two of his test was accomplished around eight thirty of that evening as Spike carried the soggy ball of fur in from the garden and placed it neatly into one of the Yorkshire blokes big shiny shoes left by the back door. Later that night as the Yorkshire bloke got ready to leave, he could hear him laughing with the blonde one in the kitchen. Apparently, they had found it rather amusing to find Spike's fur ball in his shoe. The blonde one fetched some kitchen roll and wiped it clean.

"I don't think Spike likes me," the Yorkshire bloke laughed as he put his shoes on.

"Of course, he does," the blonde one replied, "that's why he left you a little present in your shoe, think yourself lucky it wasn't a dead mouse."

Spike was frustrated by this reaction. As if he would give a fur ball as a present, only the creatures he hunted and killed counted as gifts, everyone knew that. But the final phase of his plan was the best test of all and he knew it would really try the Yorkshire bloke's patience.

Recently, Spike had been bought a basket to lie in. It was in the corner of the kitchen and he loved to stretch and sprawl out in it on his back. This exposed all of his underneath fur which was pure white and especially soft and velvety. Spike liked lying in this position but discovered that he could only really do it when no-one was around. This was because the sight of all this beautiful white fur caused his family to stroke and tickle his tummy and he really didn't like that. He would tolerate it for them and if it went on too long he would simply jump away. Several nights later, the Yorkshire bloke was back again and so Spike waited until he was about to leave. He knew he would put his shoes on in the kitchen and so he sprawled out on his back exposing his belly and the soft white fur and closed his eyes. Sure enough, the Yorkshire bloke fell straight into his trap. He could not resist bending down to massage the white velvety fur on Spike's tummy. As soon as he touched him, Spike lunged at his hand and arm with both of his front paws. He dug his claws in and bit him as well.

"OW! You bloody thing!" The Yorkshire bloke exclaimed and he threw his shoe at Spike as he ran towards the cat flap.

The blonde one was shocked to see the damage Spike had done, she grabbed Spike and stopped him from escaping.

"Look what you've done Spike, don't be so cruel," she said.

She was really cross with Spike and Spike had not felt that before.

She bathed the Yorkshire bloke's arm and kissed him good night. As she closed the door, she looked at Spike in his basket.

"I thought you were on my side," she said as she turned the kitchen light off.

Spike could see the tears in her eyes as she went to bed. He washed himself and curled up to sleep and as he drifted off, he realised that maybe he needed to trust her judgement and let her take her own necessary risks.

Chapter Six

Moving Out

"Cats fool us into thinking they are wild and oft astray

But really they like patterns and a routine for the day."

The weeks and months passed by with many ups and downs. The Yorkshire bloke was a regular visitor to the house and Spike had decided he was better off being supportive than mischievous. He had also learned a bit more information about the new man in their lives. He had two children the same age as Amy and Dan and they too were going through a difficult time. This was due to the fact that their parents had recently divorced.

But Spike could sense other changes as well, the blonde one was working extremely hard writing essays and reading books. She was doing her best to keep everything together and Spike could see just how much easier it was to have someone else to help her. There were endless tasks around the house and she was still having major problems with Dan. Dan was steadfastly refusing to co-operate, he made a huge fuss if the blonde one asked him to lend a hand, load the dishwasher or cut the grass and he point blank refused to baby sit for his younger sister. The blonde one would try her best to control him but Spike could see that whenever she fought back, she was simply playing right in to his hands; Dan wanted a fight.

One evening, she brought all of her children together, she had important news.

"I've got a job," she announced. "But it means we will have to move house, not too far away only twenty miles or so."

Spike could sense she was nervous about delivering this news. Amy showed no emotion which made Spike realise she was not hearing this for the first time.

"The thing is I have to do something. I have to provide for you all," she continued.

Claire and Dan listened intently.

"So we are off to the city. Claire, I'm sorry but you won't be moving up to the big school with all your friends but Dan, you'll be able to catch the train to finish your last year."

Spike heard her quicken the pace, she was trying to say as much as possible before the bomb went off.

"So I will be putting the house on the market and we'll start looking for a new place to live," her voice trailed off.

Spike could see this was not the full story. She jumped back in before Dan could start his tantrum. *May as well be hung for shilling as a farthing*, she thought.

"And Eric has asked me to marry him and I've said yes. So we will be looking for a new house for all of us to move into eventually... after the wedding."

There she had said it.

SLAM!!!

Dan had left the room, slamming the lounge door so hard Spike feared the house would fall down around them. The blonde one looked anxiously at her two daughters and they both smiled at her. They hugged their mother reassuringly but Spike felt the immensity of the task in front of her; nevertheless, she was determined to move on.

Spike made his way up the stairs to find Dan. He pushed the door of the front bedroom with his nose and sure enough Dan was sitting in the blue chair, his face was red with rage. Spike jumped up and Dan began to stroke his fur with repeated intent. Spike purred with pleasure and tiny wisps of black and white fur flew up into the air landing on the blue cushion of the chair. Dan said nothing but Spike could feel his anger burning through each movement of his hand as he stroked his fur. There were no tears but the room was electric with emotion and as Spike tried to absorb the woe and bring comfort slowly, the familiar scene of the front bedroom began to fade until they found themselves in a football stadium.

Spike was walking in amongst a huge crowd but Dan was nowhere to be seen. He trotted up some steps and made his way into the grounds where the spectators were taking their seats. The score board showed that this was the second half and the score was 1:1. As the game got under way, Spike looked up at the crowd from where he was standing at the side lines. He was still searching for Dan, wondering why they had been separated. The stadium was full and the noise of cheering, shouting and singing was deafening but he could not see Dan anywhere. From time to time, the singing would stop but then a big drum would beat and the supporters would begin to sing again in order to encourage their team. Eventually, Spike settled down on the grass out of the way and watched the game, he was behind the home team goal line and when the ball came near, he felt the electricity of expectation in the atmosphere and the surge of noise from the crowd.

Forty minutes into the second half, Spike suddenly caught sight of Dan. He was standing on the side lines, wearing the home teams strip with a number nine on the back of his shirt and as Spike watched, he could see that he was beginning to warm up in order to go on and play.

Eventually, the referee blew his whistle for a throw in and signalled for the substitution to take place at the same time. Dan ran onto the pitch and the crowd cheered. As the game got started, it wasn't long before Dan had possession of the ball. He passed it and ran forward towards the goal where Spike was watching, the crowd were cheering and chanting his name with the drum beating loudly, but the opposition won it back. The crowd groaned but Dan chased the player down and tackled the ball back. He turned and ran like lightening towards the goal area again. The noise of cheering surged as Spike watched Dan skilfully run with the ball, nearer and nearer he came, he passed the ball to the player on his left and ran forward; the crowd were up on their feet as they watched Dan position himself to receive the ball again. This was what they had been waiting for.

Dan was still on side as he reached the penalty area and everyone was cheering him. But just before he could score, he was mercilessly tackled and brought to the ground. The crowd went mad. Spike could see all of Dan's fellow team mates rush up to confront the player who had fouled him, they were pushing and shoving as Dan rolled on the ground in pain. Others from his team were appealing to the referee and looking at the lines man.

"Pen-al-ty, pen-al-ty," the crowd stared to chant. And sure enough the referee awarded the penalty and sent the other player off the pitch with a red card.

Dan rose from the ground and assured everyone around him he was perfectly OK to take the shot. As he stood in front of the goal, he could hear the crowd cheering but inside his head, he heard one voice as clear as could be. Spike heard it as well.

"This is your chance, make it happen," it said.

Spike watched nervously as the ball soared through the air into the back of the net. The crowd around him erupted and the noise was deafening… Dan ran towards the fans and his team mates jumped on him bringing him to the ground in mad celebration. This was the winning goal with a score of 2:1 and now, there were only 30 seconds to go. Dan had done it, he had taken his chance and made it happen.

....

It took the whole of the summer for the house to sell and for a new home to be found in the city, but now, this was their last week in the house before the move. There were boxes everywhere and the rooms of the house were strangely empty and echoey as Spike padded through each one. He was feeling a number of apprehensions wondering what the new place would be like and how he would be able to mark a new territory. He had heard alarming stories about the city from some of the cats in his neighbourhood who had related tales to him that made his eyes grow wide with dismay. They had told him about mean clever foxes who were especially talented at stripping cats of their fur before they ate them and how all the rats and tomcats were twice the size as here in the village. He tried to push his fears away and told himself he had a job to do and that the children were more important than his worries. On the last night, he curled up next to the blonde one who had unusually let him sleep on her bed. She turned and stroked him.

"Spike, I'm so glad you're here with us and I know you will love the new house."

Her voice sounded sleepy but she continued,

"The road is quiet and best of all the garden backs straight onto the woods. I think you will have plenty of birds to chase... and mice to catch, but don't bring them home." She laughed quietly.

These reassuring words were all that Spike needed, he pressed himself against her as she drifted off to sleep and decided he would spend his last night in his home right beside her.

Early in the morning, a huge lorry arrived and two men started to move everything out of the house. Things started quite positively and even Dan had gotten used to the idea. He seemed to quite enjoy helping the two men. Amy was at work and had planned to drive straight to the new house when she finished, she knew she would have to get used to this daily journey to work, so that was fine. Claire, on the other hand, was struggling. She was like a limp lettuce and, at times, even looked the same colour. She complained of feeling hot and unwell. But the blonde one didn't really have time to attend to her and besides what could she do, her bed had already been put on the lorry. Spike was sitting in the kitchen when it happened; he was looking into the hallway facing the front door. The door was open all of the time and he was trying to decide if he was safer inside or out. But just as the two men walked back into the house, Claire came running out of the lounge towards the door and vomited right in front of them. Her timing was immaculate. The men just managed to avoid walking through the large pool of sick and hastily got out of Claire's way as she ran outside. They continued to carry things to the van via the back door as the blonde one cleared up the mess. Spike ran outside where Claire was still being sick. *Poor Claire,* he thought. But Dan was thoroughly amused by it all and took his phone out in order to take pictures of Claire being sick, he was planning to show his friends later. This provoked Claire into an emotional state of meltdown and Spike watched with horror as yet again, the blonde one had to contend with the sibling rivalry whilst clearing up sick, unpacking some clean clothes for Claire and gingerly put her sick covered trousers and top into a bin liner. Eventually, she settled Claire down on the back seat of the car next to an orange bucket. *Nothing was ever easy for her,* she thought.

As the last box was loaded onto the lorry, Spike was lifted up and placed inside his basket with the cage door on the front. He felt sure the basket had shrunk, since his first journey home in it two and a half years ago. Claire was now fast asleep but Spike was placed on the back seat beside her, he could feel the warmth of her breath. Dan sat in the front seat as the car followed the large lorry up the hill away from the familiar roads of the housing estate. Dan glanced at the houses where his mates lived, they were empty, no one waved them goodbye and he remembered the day they had travelled up this road in the big black cars. That day, all of the neighbours' curtains had been drawn as a mark of respect. Today, their leaving seemed to go unnoticed. Spike tried to see out of the car window but it was difficult from inside the basket. All he could see were the clouds in the sky, and from time to time, he would catch a glimpse of the tops of trees and the roofs of buildings.

No one spoke as they travelled away from the village towards the city and although the journey didn't take long, Spike knew it would still be too far for him to ever visit his old patch again. There was a sombre air in the car and Spike wished he could be free of his cage, he wanted to sit with Dan or curl up on Claire. Even he wanted to be stroked in order to feel secure. It was as if each person in the car, although travelling together, were travelling separately with their own thoughts and it felt strange. Somehow, the twenty mile journey was taking each of them a million miles away from their old home and life.

Eventually, Spike felt the car turn sharply up a hill and begin to slow down. He looked up through the bars of his cat basket to see a line of trees, all of which had pretty pink blossoms on them. As he watched, the wind blew some of the petals up into the air, swirling them round before they fell to the ground. Spike wanted to play with them and he itched to get out of his basket.

The car stopped and everyone got out.

"Don't let Spike out of his basket until we know he is safe inside," he heard the blonde one say.

But Spike wondered if he and his family would ever feel safe again.

Chapter Seven

Settling In

"Sometimes to settle like a cat and choose our favourite place

We need to forcefully evict the strangers in our space."

The new house was considerably bigger than the old one but it had been bought so that the Yorkshire bloke and his children could move in as well in the not too distant future. The beauty of this house was that everyone could have their own bedroom; there were six bedrooms in all, one of which was downstairs with its own shower room.

Spike had counted three bathrooms in all, as well as the downstairs shower room, there was one off the blonde one's bedroom and another family bathroom on the first floor. He was surprised how quickly the chaos turned to order with boxes unpacked and furniture put in place; pretty soon, there was a feeling of familiarity. One of the neighbours knocked on the door to tell the blonde one which day the dustbin-lorry came but apart from that, the road seemed very quiet and no one really disturbed you.

However, the first two nights in the new house were not as restful as he might have hoped. Spike had slept for most of the first night in his basket which had been left at the foot of the stairs. But a strange noise disturbed his sleep. He opened his eyes and saw that it was barely light and then his ears pricked up; he could hear a faint buzzing noise. He stretched himself out of his basket and followed the noise, it was coming from upstairs. He ran up each step to investigate and realised that the noise was coming from the bedroom on the right. This was where the blonde one was sleeping and the noise was getting louder. He pushed the door ajar with his nose, the blonde one was fast asleep but Spike could clearly see the source of the noise. There was a swarm of wasps buzzing around her head. Spike leapt into action. He jumped onto her bed and started to lash out at the wasps with his paws, meowing so loudly that the blonde one woke with a start and screamed. She pulled back the sheets and grabbed Spike and ran from the room closing the door behind her. She had two wasp stings on her neck.

"Vicious things," she moaned. "Spike are you alright?" she asked as she inspected his fur. "I simply can't believe this."

She sighed and carried him downstairs to the safety of the kitchen. None of the children had heard any of the commotion but luckily, the wasps were confined to the blonde one's bedroom. Later that day, a man from pest control dealt with the wasp's nest but Spike could see that it had upset the blonde one.

For their second night's sleep in the new house, Spike decided to creep into her room and she let him sleep on her bed. It was still dark when Spike woke up but he decided to see if he had any food left in his bowl. He walked slowly and silently downstairs but as he passed the lounge door, he heard an almighty thud. Alarmed at the noise, he rushed into the lounge and there, sitting in the fire hearth, was the biggest plumpest pigeon he had ever seen. It was quite dazed from its fall and it was covered in soot. The pigeon immediately sensed the danger it was in as it caught sight of a pair of cat's eyes looking straight at it. What awful luck to survive the fall down the chimney only to be eaten by a cat and in its efforts to avoid such a fate, it began to squawk and hop and poop all over the place. The pigeon opened its wings spraying soot everywhere and tried to fly away. Spike watched intently with his tail flapping from side to side. He couldn't believe his luck. But unfortunately for Spike, the commotion brought the blonde one rushing downstairs.

"Shoo! shoo!" she said, getting herself between cat and bird.

She tried to direct the poor frightened bird towards the back door but eventually had to fetch the broom in order to coax the terrified creature outside.

"Oh Spike, whatever next," she exclaimed as she started to sweep the soot in dismay.

But Spike was already pushing himself through the cat flap into the garden. The sun was just beginning to rise but the pigeon was nowhere to be seen, all Spike found were some wet sooty marks upon the grass and the path.

The first week or two in the new house were quite busy but thankfully, there were no more disturbed nights. With the furniture in place and old familiar ornaments and belongings finding their place, Spike could see it was beginning to feel a lot like home again. He even began to identify his favourite places in this new home, one of which was the conservatory. It looked out onto the garden and was constructed out of glass, it even had a glass roof. The old house had not had one of these rooms and Spike loved it. His love was based on two factors, one being how warm the room became with the smallest amount of sunlight and the fact that there was under-floor heating which made some of the tiles wonderful places to sit. The other factor was that he could watch the birds feeding from the berries on the branches of a tall bush which partially covered the glass roof. He would climb onto the back of the conservatory couch and stretch up as far as his body allowed in order to get as near to the birds as possible. In this position, he would watch their little feathery bottoms twitching and flitting about from underneath and it drove him mad with excitement. One day, he was so mesmerised that he totally forgot there was a glass barrier between him and the birds, he threw himself forward as if to catch one only to smack his head on the glass and fall to the floor. Unbeknown to Spike, Dan had been watching him all the time. He had his hand over his mouth in case he should make a sound and disturb Spike from his venture. When Spike fell, he shouted out,

"Mum! Mum! Come and see, Spike just tried to catch a bird but forgot the glass was there, it was so funny."

Spike had landed quite safely on all four feet behind the small leather couch but he was embarrassed.

His sudden landing disturbed a rather sleepy giant moth which woke up and flew out from behind the couch straight towards Dan. If there was one thing Dan could not stand, it was moths. He had a real phobia about them. The blonde one, Amy and Claire had all run in to see the drama but now, they were watching this giant moth terrorise Dan. He screamed and ran round the room, flapping his hands up and down. Spike hardly hesitated, he leapt up and caught the offending creature in his mouth, chewed it and swallowed it.

"That's gross," Amy said and turned her face away.

"Poor moth," Claire said.

But Dan was overwhelmed with delight.

"Spike you're my hero, you saved me from that hairy moth, hooray!"

Spike strolled across the tiled floor and choosing the warmest tile, he sat down and folded his paws neatly under his body. He was proud to recover his dignity and glad to help Dan.

Dan had been finding his journey to school quite a trauma, he hated catching the bus and the train, and he made his displeasure known to all. Spike knew he was trying to get on with it but in reality, he was unable to make new friends because he was finishing his last year of big school twenty miles away. Patience was not one of his virtues either so even if he had believed all the people who kept telling him that eventually, he would make new friends and settle in, he hated waiting for it to happen.

"Why don't you try to get a part time job in the summer," his mum had suggested.

"It will get you out of the house and you'll meet people around here."

But nothing suited him, Spike would lie on his bed with him and listen to his constant rage.

"I hate living here, I hate catching buses and trains, and I miss my mates, it's all Mum's fault, why has she forced me to move away?"

Spike listened with dismay as Dan wrestled with his loyalties. What would his dad think of the new life his mother was making for herself? He felt everything was closing in on him and he didn't like the loss of control. The wedding day had been set for the following spring and that was another sore topic as far as Dan was concerned. He was negative about everything. Spike had some sympathy but he also realised that the blonde one had little choice herself but to get on with life. Every life line that was thrown towards Dan was rejected and it was this refusal to trust anything new that reminded Spike about Marmaduke.

Marmaduke was a large ginger tomcat that he had once come face to face with in a narrow alley back on his old patch. The ginger tom was extremely hostile but Spike had held his ground. They locked positions for a long time that night but eventually, Marmaduke backed down. He was injured and hungry and no real match for Spike. Spike thought he was a pathetic creature. Eventually, he discovered more about his story. The other cats had told him that Marmaduke had a problem trusting any one. When he was a kitten, he had been put into a bag and left in the river to drown. This was a frightful thing to face but fortunately, the bag had enough air trapped inside enabling him to survive long enough to be found, rescued and taken home by a little girl who then tried her best to love him. The trouble was Marmaduke simply couldn't trust her and ran away. He resorted to fending for himself and fighting to make himself look tough. He convinced himself he didn't need anyone. Sadly, a few nights after his encounter with Spike, he got into a fight with a large mother duck. Marmaduke was trying to grab her small duckling from the side of the river. The mother duck flew over him and even though Marmaduke lashed up at her with his paw, he lost his footing and fell into the river. *How ironic*, Spike thought, *that the very place from which he had been rescued ended up being his grave anyway.*

Spike shuddered and reminded himself that Dan was not alone like Marmaduke and therefore, he would not allow him to repeat poor Marmaduke's mistake of pushing every form of help away. He nuzzled into him as he played on his computer game and tried to let him know that no matter what, he was there and he would never let him down. He felt Dan relax a little and stroke his fur.

"One day, Spike, I'm going to make something happen exactly as I want it," he said.

....

Just before tea time, Amy emerged from her room and ran with some excitement down the stairs. She was looking for the blonde one to tell her the news.

"Mum, I've been accepted," she announced.

"Oh Amy, that's wonderful," the blonde one said. "Which camp?" she enquired.

"Adult Special Needs," she read from the e mail she had printed off. "I'll leave in June and return in September."

"So you're definitely here for the wedding," her mother said.

"Oh yes, no worries about that Mum."

Amy had been searching for something meaningful to do with her life. She loved the beauty therapy and although she did have a regular job, somehow, it wasn't enough. She wanted to fulfill her potential, Spike had heard her say to her mother and all this searching had led her to look at working abroad for the summer. She had been accepted for Camp America, and because she had sent her application a little late, she had not been able to choose which camp she could go to. The choice had been made for her and she was off to Iowa to a camp for Adult Special Needs. Spike could see how alike her mother she was, and he felt that she was intent on living a life now that would somehow make her dad proud.

Later that night, Spike found the blonde one sitting in the blue chair. Despite the move, it had retained a place amongst the rest of the family furniture but now instead of being in an upstairs bedroom, it was in the conservatory beside the small leather couch. The blonde one had turned the chair so she could look into the garden and turning all of the lights off, she had lit a large cream candle which gave off a pleasant aroma. It was a rare moment of quiet, Claire was asleep and Dan had returned to his computer gaming whilst Amy had driven to her friend's house to tell them her news.

Spike jumped up onto her lap, sensing her melancholy mood. As darkness fell, he watched the bushes and trees in the garden move gently in the breeze as the blonde one tickled his chin. The reflection of the candle flickered in the glass of the windows and the flames seemed to dance on the shrubs outside. As he purred, the scene began to fade until both of them were standing on a long country road.

The road was narrow and followed a gentle incline down towards a sharp bend. It was lined with trees on either side, and Spike could see the blonde one walking down the centre of it in front of him. He followed her but as they walked, the wind began to blow. At first, it was a little exhilarating but soon the temperature dropped and the sky darkened. They were in for a storm. The blonde one continued to walk down the hill towards the bend and as she did, the trees began to sway in the wind. Spike quickened his pace, sensing the closer he was to her, the safer he would be. Leaves and small branches began to fall to the ground blown by the wind and the sound of the gale grew louder as it resounded around the valley.

Still, the blonde one kept walking, she followed the bend in the road and as she continued to walk, the trees began to move more violently in the wind. Some, now, were bending almost to touch the ground and huge branches were breaking off and landing in front of her but still, she kept walking and stepping over every obstacle that fell in her path. On and on, she walked without wavering and Spike followed her. He could hear the wind intensifying and now, whole trees were crashing to the ground and landing right in front of them, but at no time were they harmed, they just kept on walking and climbing over every obstacle.

Eventually, the wind died down and Spike felt the chair bringing them back to reality. He was never quite sure how this happened but he had learned to trust the magic of the blue chair. He was simply there to guide and observe what happened, for how long and how they returned seemed to be fully within the power of the blue chair.

Now, back in the quiet of the conservatory, the blonde one sat for a few minutes with Spike curled up on her knee. He could hear her breathing softly in the darkness and the candle flickered silently.

"Spike, no matter how precarious this journey gets, I know we will survive," she whispered.

Spike felt her strength and he knew she was right.

Chapter Eight

Special Days

"But cats are quite particular about their toilet habits

They like things neat and tucked away, not scattered round like rabbits."

Spike was watching the blonde one as she pulled the long string of pretty-coloured lights out of the box. He was strangely curious of all the treasures emerging from the cardboard boxes that she had fetched from the basement. There was a huge tree inside the conservatory which the blonde one was busy decorating with tinsel and baubles and lights. She was humming and singing and quite obviously enjoying every minute of her creativity. She had fetched holly from the bush outside and was twisting it together with twine; occasionally, she would tease Spike with these long pieces of twine causing him to pounce and chase them. She laughed at his performances and Spike was surprised how much like a kitten he felt. The tree seemed to seduce him into being incredibly playful again. He could hardly resist the temptation to spar with the silver baubles as they hung from the green pine branches. He would fight with the tinsel hanging down and when everyone was out, he would climb up the tree and chew the head of the elegant angel that sat on top. There were extra candles everywhere and the smell of pine and cinnamon. Spike had watched this season come and go for the past three years, it was always the same, the house would be transformed into a tinsel grotto and the family would become even more frenzied and busy. But it would always bring an atmosphere of cheer and warmth. This year, it was mostly the same but Spike sensed that there was more tension than usual.

Eventually, when that first Christmas morning came in their new home, the blonde one was up early. She worked tirelessly preparing food, making sure everything was in place and then she laid the table. It had far more places set this year; Spike counted seven. The wedding was set for spring next year but this Christmas, they would all spend the day together and so the blonde one was anxious that everything should be perfect. The weather certainly was, Spike looked out of the conservatory window and watched the snow gently falling until the pathways glistened like diamonds. Upstairs, the blonde one was speaking to Dan outside his bedroom door.

"Are you getting dressed Dan?" she said. "We can open our presents before everyone else arrives if you like."

There was a pause. "Claire and Amy are up," she continued. She knocked on his door but there was no reply, she tried the handle but it was locked.

"Oh, come on Dan," she pleaded.

Dan had locked himself in his room; it was his silent protest.

Spike walked into the lounge where Amy and Claire were watching TV, he felt it was their way of blocking out the tension brewing upstairs. Every so often, Claire would run to the front room and look out of the window checking the driveway. She was excited about the Yorkshire bloke coming for Christmas day with both of his children. It was going to be the first time they would all gather in the house that they would all eventually live in. Spike didn't stop in the lounge, he wanted to investigate the trouble upstairs. As he approached the top stair, he could hear the blonde one speaking on the phone to her mother from her bedroom, she sounded upset.

"I don't know what to do Mum," she said. "I just want today to be happy and now, he won't come out of his room."

Spike turned towards Dan's room and scraped the door with his paw. He waited but Dan did not open the door, so instead, he sat outside and washed his bottom.

About fifteen minutes later, Claire called up the stairs.

"They're here Mum and they're carrying chairs and presents," she sounded cheerful and excited.

The blonde one had managed to compose herself and she ran down the stairs to welcome everyone. Suddenly, the hall was full of people and noise, and Spike could hear the Yorkshire bloke laughing.

"We've carried these chairs across The Roughs," he said. "We must have looked a right sight."

Spike had learned that the woods outside his garden were called 'The Roughs' by local people and the Yorkshire bloke was very much a local. His house was about a twenty-minute walk away from the new house, but it only took him ten minutes if he walked across The Roughs.

"It couldn't have been easy in the snow," laughed the blonde one. "And all these presents as well!" she exclaimed.

Spike edged towards the bannister, he wanted to be sure the Yorkshire bloke had not brought his dog, but the coast was clear. It was then he noticed the two tall children standing in the hallway next to their dad.

"Let me take your coat James," the blonde one said kindly.

James looked rather awkward and Spike noticed he hung his head down a lot. He seemed to have trouble making eye contact. It seemed to Spike that the whole family were standing in the confined space of the hall. The Yorkshire bloke and his two children were taking off wellies and coats and putting gloves on the radiator. The blonde one was trying to help, and Amy and Claire stood watching and smiling at them all. James wrestled his coat off in the tight spot and moved along the hall which enabled Spike to see the new girl. Her name was Lizzie.

Spike noted that her head was held high, she stood very close to her dad but not so much because she felt insecure more as a way of support, even protection if need be. She looked everyone in the eye. Spike felt strangely drawn to this new girl, she had an aura that quite bewitched him. Her hair was long and fair but she had tied it up with colourful bits of material. Her favourite pair of shoes were some green doc martins boots which she left by the radiator to dry, this revealed her odd socks and Spike could see that her jeans were ripped.

"Well! Welcome everyone and happy Christmas," the blonde one suddenly said.

The Yorkshire bloke reached across and kissed her in the hall.

"Let's go and open presents," Claire shouted.

Suddenly, Dan's door flew open, he was dressed. He picked Spike up and held him like a shield against his body and walked down stairs.

"Hello," he said. "Happy Christmas."

The day seemed to turn out just fine and Spike did quite well at the dinner table. He was being handed scraps of meat from all directions, Lizzie was particularly attentive and Spike felt quite besotted with her. Everyone mucked in and helped to clear away, and Dan and James enjoyed playing computer games together. There was plenty of food and drink and later as the sun went down, the Christmas tree lights looked so beautiful.

Spike was getting ready to sleep; after all, it had been a busy day. He found himself a quiet spot and curled up.

He could hear plenty of laughter and noise as the two families played board games in the front room. As he drifted off to sleep, he found himself reflecting on the words of the blonde one.

"No matter how precarious this journey gets, I know we will survive."

Spike could see just how precarious this was and yet today, he had also caught a glimpse of the potential harmony.

....

Christmas was over but the winter certainly wasn't, and Spike hated the cold. Since moving further north, the weather seemed so much harsher. He had heard the Yorkshire bloke often comment on how the new house was above the snow line.

"Up 'ere it's six foot deep and yet down in the city, there's folk wearin' flip flops," he would joke.

But it was no joke to Spike. As well as being weeks since he had checked his boundary line, his main problem was going to the toilet. He had managed to get as far as the garden gate in order to spray it with wee, and normally, he would also find a discreet spot to do his business and then bury it in the ground. But this was getting difficult as the snow was still so deep.

One night while everyone was sleeping, he was forced to take desperate measures. He poked his head through the cat flap only to hit snow straight away, it had drifted up the back door and covered his way out. Poor Spike was so desperate that first of all, he ran into the downstairs shower room and climbed into the shower tray. He carefully positioned his bottom over the plug hole and relieved himself. But that wasn't enough. Next, he climbed onto the large pot plant in the conservatory and did a pooh. He tried to cover it up but unfortunately, he left the tell tail signs of soil on the floor. The next morning, the blonde one was left with no doubts as to what Spike had been up to. She cleared the snow away from the back door, picked Spike up and dropped him into the icy drifts.

"You can't stay in all the time Spike, now find somewhere else to do your business," she said.

As much as Spike hated it, he was left with no choice but he longed to see the return of the green grass and the birds feeding from the berries over the conservatory roof. He watched every day through the window, waiting for signs of spring and sure enough, eventually, the snow melted and the green buds began to show. Trees and bushes began to change colour and tiny bulbs began to push through the hard soil bringing hope of warmer days.

Shortly after they first moved in, Spike had found and marked out a new territory and today, he was outside checking it. It stretched from the garden gate out into The Roughs. He sprayed the garden gate post and pushed himself underneath. As the bottom of the gate brushed his furry back, he thought that somehow the snow must have made it lower than usual as it was much more of a squeeze than it used to be. He ran along the bank of trees and headed down the hill spraying as he went on appropriate branches and tree stumps. Eventually, he crossed the little bridge over the stream which led him into an open field.

Across the field, he turned left which took him along the side of a steep road. It was a pleasant day in mid-April, there was no hint of rain and he could hear the new born lambs bleating in the field. At the top of the hill as the road turned to the right, Spike turned left across a farm yard. The sheep dogs would bark angrily at him but he knew they were tethered and could not reach him. Finally, Spike would reappear and cross several front gardens of the neighbouring houses before approaching the front driveway of his house. The front door had an open stone-built porch, and Spike would often jump up onto wall and sit as though he were on sentry duty. This was his daily routine.

On this particular day though, as he jumped up on to the wall of the front porch, he was constantly disturbed by many comings and goings. The blonde one and her daughters plus Lizzie all came tumbling out of the house and drove away in the car. Four bouquets of flowers arrived and then another box of flowers arrived. Then all the girls came back with the blonde one, each of them had very glamorous hair dos and beautiful tiaras fitted into place. Just as two of the blonde one's friends arrived, Spike decided to follow them inside. The house was full of activity and giggling girls so Spike decided to escape to Dan's room. He pushed the door ajar with his nose to see Dan standing in front of his mirror trying to tie a knot in his tie. Spike hesitated as he feared this task may begin to irritate Dan and cause an explosion. But Dan turned and greeted Spike warmly. He bent down and picked him up.

"Hi Spike, today is the wedding day and I'm giving Mum away," he said proudly.

He was dressed in a posh suit with top hat and tails, and Spike suddenly saw how grown up he looked. He was also acutely aware of how far Dan must have come in order to say those words,

"…I'm giving Mum away."

He pushed his face into Dan's and purred loudly. Dan pushed back, he loved Spike very much but then he placed him on his window sill and finished getting ready. Eventually, the house began to empty and become quieter and outside, Spike saw two black cars arrive. One car was for all of the bridesmaids who looked wonderful in their purple silk dresses. As they climbed into the big car, they giggled and laughed trying not to damage their bouquets of tulips. The other car waited; it was for the bride and Dan.

A few minutes later, there was a gentle knock on Dan's door, it opened slowly to reveal the blonde one; she was dressed in a long creamy white dress and Spike thought it looked as smooth as milk. Dan smiled at her and Spike sensed that they both felt the significance of the present moment as well as the sadness of the past.

From the window of Dan's room, Spike watched the two black cars carry them away and it made him think about the day he had watched a trail of black cars carry his family away once before. That was the day they all said goodbye to Dad and Spike recalled how they returned to the house with open wounds and sorrowful scars, but today, it was different. This was not about loss, this was about gain and reward and joy.

This was about making a future and multiplying. If Spike could have been present that day in church, he would have saluted the blonde one and the Yorkshire bloke, for this was a brave commitment they were making. Their love was not just a casual partnership, it was about being husband and wife, yes, it was precarious and there were no guarantees, but at least, they were all moving forward and stepping out with faith, determined to overcome every obstacle.

Chapter Nine

Early Days

*"Cats only fight to make the peace that others try
to keep*

*For sometimes only conflict can achieve such
peaceful sleep."*

The blonde one and the Yorkshire bloke enjoyed a brief
honeymoon but a week after they returned, the Yorkshire
bloke and his two children moved in. The Yorkshire
bloke had sold his house but was still waiting to complete the
transaction. This gave him the luxury of moving in slowly.

Spike watched the van arrive several times over the week and deliver piles of stuff. Both James and Lizzie had been allocated bedrooms; Lizzie was upstairs on the front and James was given the downstairs front room. Although this was not strictly a bedroom, it did mean no one had to share a room or squash into the small box room upstairs. The blonde one helped the Yorkshire bloke to clear his old house and tried her best to settle everyone in, but it was pandemonium. All of the children seemed to get on quite well initially but no one was helping. Not only that, but Lizzie seemed to have hundreds of friends all of which she wanted to show her new home to. Outside in the garden, there was a small empty stable which had been converted into a garden room. It housed a snooker table and some chairs. Lizzie thought this was a great place to hang out with all of her friends.

Back in the house, there was stuff everywhere and people seemed to be cooking and eating food all the time as well. Each time the blonde one and the Yorkshire bloke came back with more stuff, they were greeted with all the mess everyone had just left lying around. Spike spent most of his time upstairs, keeping out of the way; he felt the tension especially from the blonde one. She was struggling with the loss of control she felt over her precious home.

Eventually, the van, which the Yorkshire bloke had hired, brought the last pile of boxes and bits and pieces to the house. Spike watched the Yorkshire bloke slide the van open to start the emptying process but then, to his dismay, he saw a medium brown dog lumber down out of the van onto the pavement. She slowly ambled down the drive and Spike knew that she was moving in as well. He ran to the top of the stairs, keeping himself hidden and watched her enter his house.

"Lady," shouted the Yorkshire bloke from outside.

But she laid on the floor and ignored him.

Spike quickly deduced that she was quite old and slow, she had a funny smell like damp soil. Lady's nose was twitching, she could smell Spike but she was far too lazy to investigate.

Suddenly, the Yorkshire bloke ran in.

"Where's Spike?" he shouted.

"We're gonna have to keep 'em apart 'til they get used to each other," he said to the children sat watching TV.

Spike thought he sounded quite anxious and retreated onto Claire's bed.

For the next few days, the Yorkshire bloke was obsessed with keeping Lady and Spike well away from each other. Lizzie was quite frustrated with him.

"They'll be fine Dad," she said. "Just let them meet each other."

But every time Spike ventured downstairs, he would jump up and shut all of the doors so that Spike could only go straight through to the kitchen bypassing the lounge. It was the same if he heard the cat flap go, he would run and grab Lady by her collar until Spike had disappeared upstairs.

Spike was quite fed up by all of this fuss and besides, he missed sleeping on the settee and having the freedom to wander about. One day, he saw his chance to end his isolation.

He was sitting on Dan's window sill so he had a clear view of the front of the house and the driveway. The Yorkshire bloke was trying to unload a large flat screen television out of the back of his car. Naturally, this fully engaged both of his arms. Lady was sitting on the drive, watching him, but the front door of the house was wide open. Spike quickly jumped down and ran down the stairs. He walked through the front door onto the drive just as the Yorkshire bloke turned around. But there was nothing he could do to prevent them from meeting, he simply watched in dismay with his mouth wide open. Spike walked straight passed Lady and said,

"Morning."

Lady sniffed him and that was that.

This was quite a story at tea time, Spike could hear the Yorkshire bloke recounting the episode with full vigour; he was quite a story teller. Everyone was laughing and Lizzie said,

"I told you Dad."

Things were much better for Spike after that, Lady showed no desire to chase him at all. Spike quickly learned that her over-riding passion was for food. She was constantly on the look-out for any scraps she could find. She would lick the crumbs off the wooden floors and steal anything left lying around. When people were eating, which was a lot, she would sit herself in front of them and stare until they gave her something from their plate, she wouldn't budge an inch. Wherever there was food or the merest possibility of food, she was there.

One day, Spike was sitting on the back of the blue chair in the conservatory, he was watching Lady in the garden. He could see her pushing her way through the hedge onto next door's garden. She would do this quite regularly in order to eat the bread put out for the birds. On this occasion though, the neighbour sent her back and called over the fence. The Yorkshire bloke was just about to sit down and eat a flapjack with a cup of tea when he heard the commotion. He opened the back door and walked down the outside steps into the garden to speak to the neighbour over the fence. He was complaining that Lady had been eating the bone meal he had placed around his roses and that she was always taking the bread and the nuts he put out for the birds. The Yorkshire bloke apologised and called Lady inside. He sounded quite angry.

Lady ran straight back into the house, but as she trotted into the lounge, she eyed the flapjack on the plate on the floor. Just as the Yorkshire bloke came back into the room, without a moment's hesitation, she gulped it down in one bite. The Yorkshire bloke started to tell her off but then he just looked at her and sighed. Claire and the blonde one were helpless with laughter as Lady retired to her basket, turning her back on all of them.

Spike felt quite inspired by Lady at times. She did absolutely nothing and yet everyone doted on her. She was incredibly lazy and sometimes, she would refuse to move even if the blonde one was trying to clean up and hoover. Once, she just laid back and let the blonde one hoover all the lose fur off her body. Spike didn't really love Lady but he didn't hate her either, they just settled down together with a degree of indifference.

Things weren't so easy for the rest of the family. The blonde one really wanted to be welcoming and fair, but she was having real difficulties with the amount of extra clearing up she was having to do. These two families were so different and yet, they were having to learn to live with each other, the honeymoon was well and truly over. One main difficulty was the difference between their daily routines. The blonde one's children would wake up in the morning have breakfast and go to school or college or work. As a consequence, they would also retire to bed at a reasonable time. But Lizzie and James seemed much more nocturnal, they would stay up late and sleep late. This meant that the house was never quiet and the appliances were always on the go like the TV, the oven and the computer. When they did go to bed, they left an array of cups and plates strewn all over the lounge with pizza scraps and blobs of tomato ketchup and mayonnaise on them.

The blonde one didn't like to say anything although she certainly told her own children off if need be. Another bone of contention was that lounge door was always left open so Lady would sleep on the settee and spread her fur everywhere and the lights were left on all night as well. All sense of order had disappeared and the tension was starting to take its toll on her. The last thing she wanted to do was to blow her top; after all, they hardly knew each other and she didn't want to be typecast as the wicked step mother. The Yorkshire bloke was far less concerned and seemed to go with the flow, but that seemed to increase the blonde one's stress.

Whenever they took Lady for a walk, the blonde one would explain about the mess and the waste of electricity and the Yorkshire bloke would assure her he'd have a word. But he hated confrontation. His fear was deeper than that though, after all, his children were having a hard time as well. Their wounds were still pretty raw since their mother left them and now effectively, they had been forced to leave their home and live with another family. With this in mind, he simply didn't want to cause any more upset or criticise them. But clearly things could not go on like this.

Spike continued to watch his family through all of this upheaval but he found himself especially fascinated with Lizzie and James.

When James wasn't at school, he tended to spend most of his time in his room, his passion was gaming. Occasionally, he would venture out to collect some food from the fridge or the cupboards but mostly he kept himself to himself. Dan and James got on OK but Dan had found a new passion in golf. He spent as much time as possible up at the driving range or on the golf course. Dan had also managed to get a part time job, stacking shelves at the local supermarket, and sure enough he had made some new friends. Spike liked being in James' room, he loved the clothes on the floor and the papers spread out across the carpet. He often stretched himself out on James' floor, sleeping on his dirty socks or discarded newspaper.

He would also help himself to the half-filled cups of milky tea left on the floor and sometimes, he would lick the cheesy bits he found in old pizza boxes under the bed. James was easy going and comfortable. But his demeanour drove the blonde one mad.

"He's passively resistant," he heard her say one day.

"He's nice to everyone but he never does anything you ask of him even though he agrees with you at the time. He still hasn't emptied his bin and he never makes his bed," she complained.

"I'll do it then," the Yorkshire bloke snapped back at her.

They glared at each other and Spike felt quite alarmed.

Both of them were silent as they ate their tea but afterwards, they both disappeared with Lady into The Roughs.

Spike was not one for walking with humans or dogs but on this occasion, he decided it was vitally important that he should go. He ran down the garden and jumped over the wall, sprinting down the hill, he soon caught up with them. Lady was walking with her nose to the ground and they were crossing the bridge into the field. Spike didn't use the bridge this time; instead, he ran along the stream until there was a clearing. Sitting on the other side of the stream, he could see the couple on the field, Lady was oblivious to the row but Spike wasn't.

The blonde one was shouting and waving her finger and the Yorkshire bloke was staring at the ground. Eventually, they sat down on the grass and Spike could see that she was crying. The Yorkshire bloke tried to comfort her but she drew away. Spike was really worried, he had never seen this before and so he began to mew as loud as he could. His meowing caught their attention straight away. He looked at them and mewed even louder over and over again. They simply had no choice but to get Lady on the lead and cross the stream to where he was.

The blonde one picked him up and smiled.

"It's as if he knows," she said.

"Aye, he doesn't like it when we fight, and neither do I," the Yorkshire bloke said and he put his arms out and pulled her close. Spike liked being hugged between them.

"We mustn't let these early days get the better of us," he whispered.

"We'll only make things worse, I know it seems grim but time will heal and change things, and I know we'll be alright."

Somehow, the row had cleared the air and thanks to Spike, all was calm again. They wandered back up the hill to the house and drew the curtains. The dishwasher still needed emptying but they did it together. And Spike climbed into his basket and washed his furry body from his bottom to his head.

....

As the weeks went by, Spike decided that he wanted to show his gradual acceptance of the Yorkshire bloke into the family by leaving him a special gift. The Roughs provided the perfect hunting ground and what's more Spike didn't have to venture too far to make a catch.

He would often crouch down low just under the garden gate, there were so many bushes and trees and long grass that sooner or later he knew some poor mouse would suddenly dart out. Spike waited and sure enough, he heard a noise and saw a mouse running straight past him; with one swipe of his paw, the creature was lifeless. Spike carried it back to the house, it was just before dawn, and he went straight into the hall where the Yorkshire bloke usually left his briefcase ready for work. It was wide open so Spike popped the dead mouse in and wandered back into the kitchen to finish his food from the night before. This now meant he had to jump onto the kitchen side as any food left on the floor was devoured by Lady. It was quite a jump for him these days but he usually managed to scramble up. He ate the left overs and jumped down in order to find a spot in the lounge to curl up and sleep.

He dozed until breakfast time, he liked to be around as everyone got ready to leave the house and he didn't want to miss being fed. But he especially liked waiting for the Yorkshire bloke as he always saved the last bit of milk in his cereal bowl for him. Spike liked this as it was milky and sweet with sugar. Everyone was rushing around this morning, Amy was searching for her car keys, Dan was wanting a lift from her, the Yorkshire Bloke was putting his sandwiches inside his briefcase and fastening it and the blonde one was putting her coat on. He then watched them all pour out of the house onto the drive closing the door behind them, but then just as quickly they all ran back in. They all stood huddled together in the hall watching the pavement through the window of the front door. Spike pushed through the cat flap and ran round to the front of the house. As he got there, he could see the reason why his family had retreated back into the hall. A little old man was walking past with his old black poodle, they both walked very slowly but the little old man loved to talk.

Spike remembered once when the blonde one had told them all how she had got caught in conversation for half an hour with this little old man and no matter how hard she had tried she couldn't get away, it had made her late for work. The Yorkshire bloke had also fallen victim to this and so now, they were all inside waiting for him to pass by. As he disappeared around the corner, Spike heard Amy's voice,

"Coast is clear," she called back to the rest of them.

"Gosh, I feel awful," the blonde one said to her, "but I can't be late this morning".

They all got into their separate cars and drove away; inside, Spike noticed the Yorkshire bloke had forgotten to pick up his briefcase.

Chapter Ten

Goodbye Lady

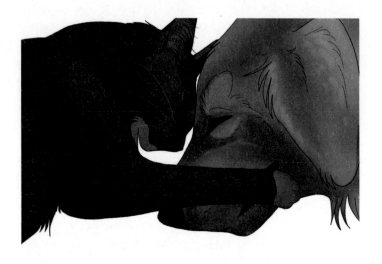

"Cats only walk beside you so you will not feel alone

They're not like dogs who need a lead, an owner and a bone."

Spike woke up in the blue chair, it was early morning and Dan was getting his stuff ready for his golf tournament, the blonde one was making his sandwiches and Claire was walking downstairs in her horse riding gear. Although it was the weekend, the blonde one was still just as busy giving lifts. Claire went down into the basement to fetch her boots, she carried them upstairs to the kitchen before carefully tipping them upside down and giving them a shake. Suddenly, a large spider fell from inside one of her riding boots and Claire screamed.

The spider was huge and it ran across the kitchen floor into the conservatory where Dan was practising his swing; he liked to do this in the conservatory as the windows gave him a 360 degree reflection.

"Dan I've told you not to swing your golf clubs in the house," the blonde one shouted.

"Watch out for the spider!" Claire exclaimed.

Spike followed the spider with his nose to the ground, the spider stopped and Spike saw his chance. He stood directly over the spider and dropped himself on top of it.

"Spike's squashing it," Dan said with great amusement.

Spike folded his paws neatly under his body and sat as still as a stone.

Claire smiled at Spike and cautiously put her boots on.

"Come on, lets go," the blonde one called from the front door.

Claire spent most of Saturday up at the farm riding horses and helping out, she loved being there and Spike could smell the horses and hay on her clothes when she came home. Dan had found a real passion for golf and these days if he wasn't playing, he was practising. He would spend hours in the garden hitting little plastic balls into the Roughs as well as a good few clumps of grass. Spike had even seen him hitting proper golf balls over the garden wall into the trees when no one was in.

Eventually, he was found out though as one of the neighbours came round with one of Dan's golf balls to complain. He was quite angry, as it had nearly hit him whilst he sat in his garden. Spike thought Dan seemed a lot happier when he was being competitive, well, as long as he won. If he lost, everyone knew about it, it was as if a door flew open and all the anger and rage would surge out. Spike would try to console him but Dan was still so fragile and the whole family were affected by the tension he created.

By mid-day, everyone except James was out and the house was strangely quiet. Spike pushed his way into his room. James sat on his computer chair with the duvet wrapped around him, his hair was all dishevelled and despite no real wash or breakfast or getting dressed, he was already engrossed in a game. Spike sniffed beside the bed, he could smell cheese so he pushed his head under the bed and found the remains of a midnight sandwich. He licked up the cheesy bits and pushed himself further under the bed looking for a warm spot to sleep, it was then that he saw the box.

His natural curiosity made him look inside, the first thing he saw was an old photograph album, it was open and Spike could see James standing between his mum and his dad in front of a Christmas tree, he was smiling broadly. Another picture showed him hugging Lady on a green leather settee next to Lizzie and the last picture he could make out in the dim light showed James in the snow holding a pair of skies leaning against his dad. Spike felt as though he had stumbled across a forgotten world, a world within which James had lived and thrived, and now, he was just a shadow of himself. It made him realise how little he had seen James smile and he certainly couldn't imagine him displaying the kind of energy that's needed to ski down a mountain. It made him realise how lost James was since his mum had left.

Over the weeks, Spike had observed James lumbering around the house displaying little or no care of himself and although he never complained, every ounce of his body language shouted out,

"What's the point?"

He would drop himself untidily onto a chair or his bed, sometimes, he would fall asleep on the settee and Spike would think he looked like a huge tree that had fallen down with his arms and legs sprawling and his mouth wide open taking up all the space. There was nothing tidy about James. Claire seemed to get on well with him though, if she ever caught him sleeping like this, she would jump on him and tickle him. James would giggle uncontrollably and play fight with her, but he was always gentle and Spike would catch a glimpse of the boy that had somehow disappeared. Spike walked out from under the bed and pushed himself against James but he couldn't really feel Spike through the duvet cover.

Just then, the house phone rang. Lizzie had just walked in so she answered it; after a brief conversation, she called to her brother.

"Mum's on the phone."

James sighed and got up, he picked the phone up and grunted, there was no energy or excitement, he hardly responded. The whole conversation consisted of James listening and grunting, Spike had even seen him put the phone down mid conversation and watch TV, he would then occasionally pick the phone back up to grunt pretending he had been there all the time. *This was his way of punishing her*, Spike thought. Spike felt a surge of compassion for both of these new children and he wondered how he might help them, how were these two families with all of their broken bits ever going to heal and become one. *It was impossible*, Spike thought, and he wondered if he would ever be able to lead them to the magic of the blue chair.

....

Spike's favourite time of day was early evening, especially if everyone was home. He loved to jump up onto someone's lap and be fussed, Lady wasn't allowed on the settee and would often settle in her basket so there was no competition. It was mid-summer now and the evenings were full of light but as Spike came into the lounge, all he could see were the dirty discarded dinner plates the children had left on the settee and Lady was helping herself to the scraps. The blonde one was working late but Spike knew she would not be happy at this scene. The Yorkshire bloke had been away for a couple of nights and so all of the household chores were left to her. Spike heard the front door as the blonde one came in, she stopped at the bottom of the stairs and called,

"Has anyone walked the dog?"

No one replied and Spike heard her sigh heavily. As she passed Jame's room, she closed his door, she always did this, it was her only way of blocking off the mess. Seeing the mess in the lounge, she headed straight to the kitchen and picked up the dog lead.

"Come on Lady, I'll take you."

Lady wagged her tail and the pair of them set off, suddenly Spike decided to join them. He pushed through the cat flap and jumped over the garden wall, at the top of the bank, he meowed to get the blonde one's attention. She stopped and turned and waited. Spike ran down to them.

"Ah! Spike how nice, are you coming too," she laughed.

It wasn't a long walk as Lady grew tired quite easily, but Spike made the most of it. He ran along beside them, showing off his agility by running across branches and climbing trees. The blonde one couldn't quite believe that Spike was walking with them as well and it greatly amused her. *Who's taking who for a walk*, she thought. But Lady was oblivious and just sniffed the ground. Eventually, they completed the circuit and headed back up the hill.

Even Spike got a bit out of breath as he trotted up the hill with Lady and the blonde one. He had noted that he was far less inclined to wander far from the house these days, as he preferred the safety of the garden. The main reason for this was a recent close encounter with a fox. One night, Spike was about a mile away from his house, hunting when all of a sudden, he became the hunted one. He froze as he caught sight of the two eyes looking at him. He hadn't heard a thing but there in front of him was a large fox grinning and licking its lips. Fortunately, they were close to a road and the fox was startled by the noise of a car speeding round the bend. Spike grabbed his chance and ran all the way home. He saw little point in hunting after that, especially as he and Lady had learned how to fuss their family in order to get all kinds of treats and left-overs from their plates. Once, Spike recalled how Dan, the blonde one and then James had all given him breakfast on the same morning just because he made a fuss round them when they came in to the kitchen.

"Three breakfasts Spike," Dan had said when he found out.

"No wonder you're so fat,"

The thing was that he wasn't the only one to say it, Spike had heard it many times from all kinds of visitors.

"Wow! Your cat is enormous," they would exclaim.

Spike thought it was quite rude, but he did have increased trouble jumping onto the kitchen side and running up hills, but no-one spoke about diets so he didn't really mind.

....

It was three days later when the Yorkshire bloke eventually returned, Spike heard everyone laughing in the lounge and he also heard his name.

"Spike had only gone and left a headless mouse in me briefcase," he heard the Yorkshire bloke say.

"I could smell somit funny and, I thought, have my sandwiches gone off? But they were fine, so I emptied everything out, and this is in front of my clients. Couldn't believe it when a mouse fell out," he was smiling and chuckling as he relayed the story so Spike felt quite safe to enter the room.

All the children were there enjoying the story and Dan picked Spike up proudly.

"Well," said the blonde one.

"The other night, he came on a night time walk with me and Lady, I'm sure he knows when I'm stressed. But he just followed us all the way round jumping into trees and running across branches as though he was trying to cheer me up, and it certainly did the trick."

As the family talked and laughed and shared their news, they fussed over Spike. He felt like a king as he lapped up their praise and he purred like a train.

Later that night, Spike was feeling energised so he decided to check the boundary line of his territory, he was still a little cautious after the fox incident but that had happened when he had wandered further away than usual. As he made his way back towards the house, he felt relieved he had not encountered anymore foxes. He ran up the garden steps and pushed himself through the cat flap but as he entered the house, he could hear a strange noise. Spike listened intently; it was coming from Lady's basket.

Spike ran towards her as he could see she was laid on her side, twitching and whining loudly. Immediately, he ran upstairs and scratched repeatedly on the Yorkshire bloke's and the blonde one's bedroom door, it wasn't long before they both dashed passed him downstairs to see Lady. The noise she was making was quite loud now. Spike followed them into the kitchen, the Yorkshire bloke was holding Lady in his arms but there was nothing he could do. The blonde one was on the phone to the vet but Lady slowly slipped away as she put the phone down. Both of them held the limp body of Lady and sobbed. The noise woke the children and soon, all of them were round her, crying and stroking her for one last time.

Spike ran outside, he couldn't bear to see them all so distressed and he too felt the deep sadness of loss. He pushed himself under the garden gate and sat at the top of the bank in the moonlight. He remembered the walk he had taken with Lady and the blonde one, and he felt glad. *So this is how it feels to lose someone,* he thought, *how would they all cope with this on top of everything else?*

It was close to dawn when he re-entered the house and he could see straight away that James was sat in the blue chair, crying. Spike seized his chance and leapt onto his knee, James stroked him and Spike felt his tears on the back of his fur. As Spike nuzzled into James, the familiar scene of the conservatory began to fade and both of them were stood at the entrance of a fair ground.

James picked Spike up and made his way through crowds of young people and families. Small children were eating toffee apples and coaxing their dads to win a gold fish for them by knocking coconuts off a shelf. There were merry go rounds turning elegantly to the distorted sound of pipe organ music and waltzers twisting to the sound of heavy rock. But James kept on walking, for he had one ride in mind and as they turned the corner, there it was: the ghost train. There was no queue and so James walked straight through the gate and sat down in an empty carriage, putting Spike beside him. Spike sensed that although James was excited about the ride, he didn't want to be alone.

As they settled into their seats, the carriage jerked and then set off, the first few metres of the ride was in day light but around the first bend, the train disappeared into a dark tunnel and gathered speed. James blinked in the blackness and Spike's pupils grew large as he strained to see. It was a strange sensation and gave the illusion of flying through the air. As they raced through the darkness, an eerie smoky mist hung in the air and James gripped Spike tightly as though he anticipated trouble. Sure enough the next minute, an array of bright images leapt out in front of them. Some of the images were contorted faces laughing or screaming, some were objects like cricket bats, Christmas trees or snowboards. There was even a bunk bed that came flying towards them. Each time James would scream thinking they were going to crash and then he would giggle as each obstacle would disappear or the train would simply go straight through it. Eventually, the train started to pull up a steep hill, neither

James nor Spike could see how far away the top was. The hill got steeper and steeper and both of them worried they might fall out of the carriage, James held onto Spike and then suddenly, it was as if the ground beneath them had moved. Spike could feel his fur flapping in the wind and his stomach lurched. James was screaming and giggling all at the same time. The train twisted and turned round countless bends but it was exhilarating. Eventually, they began to see light at the end of the tunnel and the train began to slow down. As the track evened out, James and Spike could hear a voice.

"All change, all change," it said with authority.

As the train left the tunnel, the light hit them and they blinked hard.

"Time to change," the voice commanded and they climbed out of the carriage.

Suddenly, the magic was over and they were back in the conservatory.

The sun was rising and casting a golden light across the garden. James stood up out of the chair and stroked Spike's head lovingly. He walked into the kitchen and made breakfast for Spike and himself before getting back into his bed.

....

The days and weeks which followed Lady's death were a time of gentle grief and remembering. Spike felt the family was conscious of the empty basket and the redundant dog lead hanging on the hook in the kitchen. Spike, however, was starting to enjoy the fact that he no longer had to jump onto the kitchen side to eat his food or worry if he decided to leave something in his dish for later in case Lady might eat it. He was also getting used to sleeping in Lady's basket, it was roomy and comfortable. *Yes,* he thought, *a house is much better without a dog.* And although he had nothing against Lady, he decided that they had been rather an awkward pair.

Chapter Eleven

Making It Work

"The cat that shows us wisdom has both patience and broad mind

Resisting natural urges, they are noble, they are kind."

Although Lady had not been replaced, Spike was increasingly aware of a growing array of new pets and animals in the house. This was largely due to Lizzie's passion for animal welfare. She simply had to rescue any stray or unfortunate creature that came her way. As a consequence, she now had a large cage in her room which housed two rats. One was called Rizzla and the other Bones.

Bones was a sorry sight, he was pure white and totally blind but Rizzla was brown and exceedingly cocky. Every time Spike came into Lizzie's room, Rizzla would hiss at him and hang upside down. If Spike glared at him through the bars of his cage, he would stick his tongue out at him. He had absolutely no respect for Spike. Lizzie adored him though and she would carry him on her shoulder or inside the hood of her dressing gown as she wandered round the house. Sometimes if Lizzie sat on the settee next to Spike, Rizzla would jump out of the hood and startle him. Bones wasn't allowed out of his cage due to the fact that he was blind but Lizzie made sure he was well cared for. It had been a bit of a battle getting her dad to agree she could keep another rat.

"But they're going to put him down if they can't find a home for him Dad," she pleaded.

Spike could see the Yorkshire bloke was on a hiding to nothing as he could never say no to Lizzie. She wrapped him round her little finger ever time. But that wasn't all. Spike also had to put up with the fact that Claire had a smaller cage in her room which housed a golden hamster called Harry.

Harry lived like a king much to Spike's irritation. He was surrounded with soft bedding and was fed and watered every day. But all night long, he would run himself stupid on a wheel that squeaked and rattled in the most annoying way. One night, Spike thought he might put a stop to Harry's noise.

He crept into Claire's room while she was sleeping and tried to lift the door open on the top of the cage. Harry stopped running in his wheel immediately.

Spike lifted the door and stared down into the sawdust palace, he was contemplating his next move carefully when Claire turned over in her bed and caught sight of Spike.

"Spike no!" she shouted.

Spike ran down the stairs and sat in the hall, he licked his paws and waited. Claire turned over and went back to sleep not realising that Harry's cage was still open. It wasn't long before Spike heard furious scampering noises coming from upstairs. Harry was making the most of his new found freedom and was running across the landing in and out of all the bedrooms. Harry did everything at top speed, he found it impossible to walk anywhere. Spike stretched himself out and let his claws protrude and then he started his quiet ascent stair by stair until he emerged onto the landing. Unlike Harry who had to do everything at top speed, Spike was much more patient and measured and so he sat on the top stair and waited.

He could hear Harry as he scurried under the beds, occasionally, the noise would stop as Harry climbed the curtains and then he would hear a scraping noise as Harry let himself slide back down the curtains to the floor. Then the furious scampering noise would sound again. This repeated several times. Harry was clearly having a whale of a time, it was so much better than going round and round in his wheel. Spike decided that the next time Harry climbed the curtains would be his last, his plan was to pounce on him as he scurried past. Sure enough, he heard the sound of scraping once more and he positioned himself just inside the bathroom door. He crouched down low and as he waited he felt a tinge of excitement which made his bottom twitch from side to side; the hunt was on. He waited and waited but all sound of Harry had disappeared; eventually, Spike crept from room to room but Harry was nowhere to be seen.

Spike was most put out to be outwitted by a hamster. But the morning revealed the true story. Whilst Claire and the blonde one were frantically searching for the escapee, they discovered him at the bottom of Claire's waste paper bin.

"How ever did you get in there Harry!" Claire exclaimed.

The waste paper bin was directly beneath her curtains, fortunately for Harry, he had slightly miscalculated his final descent of Claire's curtains, accidentally landing in the bin. The next evening as Spike walked past Claire's room, Harry was running round and round in his wheel again and there was a large book on top of his cage covering the door.

That hamster has as many lives as a cat, Spike thought to himself. It had only been two weeks ago that Harry had fallen into a mug of hot chocolate. Claire had brought him downstairs and was letting him run round on the coffee table. She placed her mug carefully on the floor and turned to glance at the TV. As she did there was plop! Harry had walked right off the edge of the table, landing in Claire's mug. Fortunately, she had put lots of cold milk in so it wasn't too hot. Claire screamed and cried as she thought she had drowned him in hot chocolate but Harry just licked himself all day, enjoying every drop.

As the months passed by, the children learned increasingly how to accept each other and tentative friendships began to be forged. Spike could see that Lizzie felt quite protective towards her younger step sister Claire, and their relationship flourished around their common interest in animals. Lizzie would invite Claire to visit Meesha, the horse her parents had owned before they split up. It was stabled a few miles away and Lizzie now looked after it with her mother. Claire loved helping out. They would also clean the rats and the hamster cages out together and come up with all sorts of plans to enhance their pet's freedom. One day as Spike laid at the top of the driveway in the sun, he saw both Lizzie and Claire fixing a small ferret harness to Harry the hamster so that they could take him for a walk to the shops. Spike watched as they walked up the street with Harry running along the grass verges on his lead and Rizzla sitting as proud as punch on Lizzie's shoulder; it was a comical sight.

But Spike still found it hard to accept the fact that rodents were living in his house; after all, these were the very creatures he would hunt at night and take pride in ridding his family of. He was vastly irritated by it. However, Spike realised he had to keep his hostile feelings to himself for Lizzie and Claire were very protective of these second class pets.

As for the other children, Spike observed that although Amy was not home a great deal these days, when she did appear, she got on with everyone. Dan and James also seemed to get along OK; they didn't spend much time together but when they did, they were usually playing computer games. Dan always managed to make James laugh a lot although, sometimes, it was at the expense of Claire. Interestingly, Dan never made trouble if Lizzie was around, it was as if he knew she wouldn't stand for any of his nonsense. But Spike had detected that there were some real tensions between Lizzie and James.

Spike had often witnessed Lizzie's change in character, she would suddenly erupt with temper and direct most of it in her brother's direction. His lack of reaction only made her worse. She would accuse him of anything and everything. If her food went missing from the fridge, James had eaten it, if she lost anything, James had taken it. Spike could see that there was a tide of frustration within Lizzie itching to come out. She would goad James into arguments if she could, just to feel some relief. She was constantly torn between supporting her dad in his new life whilst coming to terms with her own losses. In reality, her anger was towards her mother for leaving them, but she wasn't there to rage at, so James got it.

It was a Friday morning when things came to a head. The blonde one was upstairs working at her desk and apart from Lizzie and James, everyone else was out. Downstairs, James was sitting, watching TV in the lounge and Lizzie was searching for her phone. Spike quickly realised that Lizzie thought she was alone with her brother. She was huffing and puffing and slamming drawers and cupboard doors in her attempts to locate her phone and then she turned on James.

"WHERE IS IT?" she screamed at him. James shrugged his shoulders, this infuriated her even more. "I know you've taken it," she accused. Lizzie walked right up to him and yelled in his face. "GIVE IT BACK NOW!" she screamed.

The row brought the blonde one downstairs and Lizzie looked shocked.

"What's wrong Lizzie, can I help?" the blonde one asked gently. Spike could sense she was anxious but James hurried away, glad to be rescued.

"I can't find my phone," Lizzie answered quietly.

"I'll help you look, let's try the back of the settee first," the blonde one said as she started to throw all of the cushions on the floor. Sure enough the phone was tucked down the side of the cushions and what's more, it was the side furthest away from where James had been sitting.

Lizzie retreated to her room whilst the blonde one replaced all the cushions and made a cup of tea. Taking a deep breath, she walked upstairs and knocked on Lizzie's door.

"Come in," Lizzie said, she was crying.

Spike ran up the stairs to join them and jumped onto Lizzie's bed, the blonde one sat down beside her.

"What's wrong Lizzie?" she asked carefully,

"I just feel so strange," Lizzie began.

"I don't mean to be unkind but I feel like a guest in this house, I have a Mum and a Dad but living here, I feel like I have an Aunt and an Uncle. I'm trying to get on with it and adjust but I miss my old life and my old bedroom."

The blonde one put her arm around her as she continued tearfully, "I want to be good for Dad but sometimes, I feel like screaming."

"I'm sorry for your pain right now, Lizzie" the blonde one replied. "It's going to take time for all of us to adjust and for things to feel normal again, but talking about your feelings is really important, don't bottle things up," she advised.

"I know," said Lizzie, " I've got loads of good friends to talk to as well."

"Good," replied the blonde one. "And don't be so hard on your brother, he's finding it hard to adjust as well," she added.

They smiled at each other and the blonde one left the room, sensing it was time to back off.

Spike stretched himself out on Lizzie's bed and purred, he turned over and pressed himself into Lizzie's hand so that she would pet him. As she stroked him, he felt her calm down and the tears stopped flowing. Spike really liked Lizzie's room, it wasn't exactly untidy but it showed artistic flare. There were coloured beads and feathers hanging from the ceiling and wind chimes in the window that gently chimed as the breeze blew in. There were tapestries on the wall and sketch books piled high beside the bed along with different coloured chalks and crayons and paint brushes. His favourite place of all was on top of her chest of drawers, for here Lizzie had laid out a long piece of bright pink fur. Spike loved to lay on this, especially if the sun was shining onto it through the window. As Lizzie calmed down, Spike made his way from the bed onto the window sill and jumped gracefully onto the pink fur. He stretched out and purred softly.

"Ah! Spike it takes a real man to admit he likes pink," Lizzie laughed.

....

Slowly, over the weeks, since Jame's episode with the magic of the blue chair, Spike could see that he was trying to come out of his shell. He had applied for university and started to attend his sixth form classes more regularly, he even started to complete his homework. Somehow, he was responding to the voice that had commanded him to change. But Spike was still worried about Dan. Even though he had managed to get himself an apprenticeship at a garage and was learning how to be a mechanic, he was still very volatile and unpredictable. Having recently passed his driving test, he now wanted a car, and not just a normal safe car, a fast expensive car. But there was a problem, he was too young to get the insurance he needed. This led him to badger his poor mother to not only insure a car in her name and add him on, but he also wanted her to take out loans so he could buy the car in the first place. Spike could hear them argue when no one else was in and Dan was so demanding and unreasonable.

Clearly he thought she owed him for all the upheaval of moving and re-marrying and at times, it was hard for her to say no, she was simply worn down by his constant asking and demanding. If she did say no, Dan would wait until no one else was around and he would whisper in her ears about how much he hated every one and how the family had been spoiled by her. It was a real trial at times. In the end, Dan settled for a small car to get him to work and back but it didn't stop him punishing his mother whenever he saw the opportunity.

One afternoon, the blonde one came home with a load of shopping, she had quickly nipped out in Dan's car as her own car was in the garage; as she stepped into the hall with her hands full of shopping bags, Dan came to the top of the stairs.

"Who said you could take my car!" he shouted angrily.

"I only went to the super market for half an hour," the blonde one replied, "I knew you didn't need it."

"Well, you owe me money now cos you've used my fuel," he retorted.

The blonde one turned and faced him, she was losing her cool now.

"Actually, I filled it up with fuel for you but I wish I hadn't. Now, HOW DARE YOU BE SO RUDE!"

Dan disappeared into the bathroom to have a shower, having pressed all of her buttons, he now walked away.

The blonde one marched into the kitchen, her face was like thunder. The Yorkshire bloke carried on unloading the car and Claire started to unpack the bags in the kitchen, she had just taken a six pack of mixed yoghurts and a carton of cottage cheese out of one of the bags and placed them on the kitchen table. Spike watched as the blonde one reached for the yoghurts but instead of placing them in the fridge, she drew her arm back and hurled them at the kitchen wall with all of her might. The Yorkshire bloke and Claire were rigid with shock. And then, she picked up the cottage cheese and hurled that as well. The walls were covered with yoghurt and cheese. For a moment, the blonde one savoured the satisfaction of her act and then she turned on Claire and the Yorkshire bloke.

"Right, get out all of you so I can clean this mess up," she commanded, they retreated hastily and she cleaned the kitchen from top to bottom in order to appease her anger. Spike stayed behind to help her by licking as much cheese and yoghurt as he could from the floor.

Spike could see how much both the Yorkshire bloke and the blonde one worked to keep things together, they did all of the chores inside and out, they both worked full-time, they shopped at least twice a week to feed everyone, they cooked, cleared up and gave lifts to everyone where ever they wanted to go. This put a constant strain on their relationship but the blonde one was not going to let things slip. Spike saw her open her diary every week and say to the Yorkshire bloke,

"Right! Which night are we going out love?"

They never missed it, and it was a good job, for without such time and care to their own relationship, they could have easily drowned in all the tension and chaos.

Spike could see that at some point, all of his new family had times when they would buckle under the pressure. But he never saw the Yorkshire bloke lose his cool with any of the children. Spike greatly admired this and he even felt a little guilty about the times he had bitten and scratched him. Spike sensed the Yorkshire bloke had a real inner strength and he knew it was similar to the magic that the blue chair offered. He had faith that things would turn out OK and he never questioned his commitment to love and to honour the vows he had made. But he also looked to a greater source of love and power to help and guide him each day and it was this humility that seemed to make the difference. The blonde one was of the same mind and it was this mutual attitude that helped them to grow together and overcome the constant pressures and obstacles.

Many times if Spike sat on the blonde one's knee during the evening, she would stroke him and whisper,

"Spike no matter how precarious this journey gets, I know we will survive."

The magic of the blue chair was alive in her and it gave her courage. However, Spike would make a hasty retreat if he saw the Yorkshire bloke carrying his tool box up from the basement to do some DIY.

The Yorkshire bloke would start off confident and cheerful, lining his tools up and singing along to the radio but then the scolding would start. As patient as he was with people, the Yorkshire bloke was as impatient with things. If he was making something or mending something, he would try to follow the instructions but invariably, it would go wrong, so then he would begin to blame the very tools he had lined up to help him. It was as if he genuinely believed they were ganging up on him. Screws and nails were thrown aside and dismissed for being awkward and uncooperative, hammers and drills were ignorant and incompetent, the wire that wouldn't thread into place was mocking him, the tile that wouldn't cut in a straight line was asking for trouble and the BBQ that he was trying to light was out to get him. Once, Spike walked into the conservatory to find the whole family laughing uncontrollably as they watched the Yorkshire bloke outside ranting at a broom. He was holding the handle in one hand and the head in the other. He had been sweeping the rain off the outside steps when, due to his heavy handedness, the broom had broken apart. Nevertheless, it was the broom that was being blamed for its disobedience. He would hurl things and swear and everyone would keep their distance but these tantrums never lasted long and provided the family with many stories to recount.

"That Bloody hammer," they would mock and giggle and the Yorkshire bloke would laugh loudly and shake his head.

Later that day when all was calm again after the throwing of the yoghurt and cottage cheese, Spike wandered out into the garden. It was getting dark and the moon was becoming visible and as he went to his favourite bush to relieve himself he reflected on the day's events. Despite the tensions and the tantrums, despite the genuine hardship of learning to blend, there was real hope that his family would stay together and Spike felt it every time he heard them laughing and recounting stories about each other. He wondered how they kept going at times but he knew that the magic of the blue chair was helping. After all, it was the blue chair that had shown him his purpose and changed him from an ordinary cat into a cat with purpose. He thought about Claire and her experience of the blue chair, *would she ever need to go again?* Or was that one encounter with the man on the bike enough to give her peace. *Time would tell*, he thought.

As he thought about Claire, he buried his pooh, licked his bottom clean and decided to sleep in her room. He made his way up the stairs and pushed her door open. Jumping onto her soft duvet cover, he stretched himself out on her bed and drank in the peace and quiet. But as he started to doze, a distant rattle and squeak irritated his ears as Harry climbed into his wheel.

Chapter Twelve

Rosie and Spike

***"Nine lives are given to the cat who doesn't
look behind***

***But keeps on moving forward, embracing each
new find."***

The blonde one sat next to the Yorkshire bloke on the settee. It had been a long day but now, the house was calmer and quieter. She leaned against him and he put his arm around her. Whenever he hugged her, she felt as though she was in a safe refuge.

"I miss the dog… and the walks," she said quietly.

"Aye me too," he replied.

Spike was laid on the floor with his hind leg held high, he was busy licking it but these words made him freeze.

"Let's go this weekend to the rescue place in the city centre," the Yorkshire bloke suggested, "I think the time is right now."

The blonde one nodded and smiled. She closed her eyes and rested on his broad shoulders. But Spike was most alarmed. He thought through the implications, Lady had been old and slow, but a new dog, that could mean anything, was no one thinking of him? But when the news broke that they were getting a new dog, the children were all incredibly excited so he knew there would be no stopping them. This led Spike to do a lot of sulking outside in the garden. Claire wandered outside to see him, but he jumped over the wall and disappeared.

"I think Spike is cross with us," she said to Dan.

"Don't be stupid," he sneered.

But she was right. That's exactly how Spike was feeling, cross. He simply couldn't understand why they should want or need a dog. Surely, he was enough for them and besides, he didn't cause half as much work. But no amount of sulking could change their minds.

Two weeks later, Spike was sitting on Dan's window sill, watching the front of the house when he witnessed the arrival of the new dog. She was wagging her tail furiously and bouncing up and down as everyone came to greet her. She was medium in size with ginger fur, although the fur under her chin was white. Her ears were velvety and floppy but she looked quite skinny. Lizzie wasted no time in running upstairs to find Spike; this time, she was going to introduce them straight away as she didn't want a repeat of her dad's paranoia with Lady. The door of Dan's room was open and so Lizzie walked over to Spike and gently lifted him over her shoulder to carry him down stairs. Spike did not feel sure about this at all. He would have preferred to introduce himself on his own terms when he felt safe and ready. Lizzie felt his body tense up and his claws cling onto her as she entered the lounge. Everyone was there including the new dog and she was running from one family member to the next, panting and licking and wagging her tail. Spike tried to wriggle free but Lizzie was not going to be stopped.

"It's alright Spike," Lizzie reassured him. Luckily, she had a good instinct for these kinds of things.

"Come and say hello to Rosie."

Lizzie was wise enough not to put Spike down but she lowered herself onto the settee and let Rosie sniff him. There was no hint of danger; in fact, Rosie licked Spike and trotted off. It was as if Rosie was just as grateful to Spike as she was to the rest of her new family for rescuing her.

Spike quickly learned that Rosie was just as daft as most of the dogs he had ever met. She was fascinated with sticks and balls and loved to wrestle with pieces of rope. She wasn't fierce or angry at all, she was a big ball of love and everyone embraced her. Occasionally, Rosie would chase Spike in the garden but Spike could jump into a tree in order to escape. However, he soon realised that Rosie was just desperate to play. She would repeatedly lower her head and front paws to the ground in front of Spike as an invitation to have some fun. Spike would try and box her face with his paws, although he never extended his claws. But Rosie would just imitate him thinking he was playing with her. Claire thought it was really funny.

"Look Rosie is copying Spike," she would call.

Actually, Spike quite liked to box Rosie's face and he took to hiding round corners in the house in order to take her by surprise. But Rosie never got angry. Spike also liked to steal Rosie's place in her basket, he would wait until she vacated it and climb onto the warm spot she had left behind. But although there was room for two, Spike would spread himself out as much as he could so there was no room for her to get back in. This didn't stop Rosie though, she would push her way back in and snuggle up close to Spike. Secretly, Spike liked it, it made him feel even more warm and cosy and the whole family loved it when they shared the basket together.

"It's like a little sign of harmony," the blonde one said.

What Spike had expected and dreaded about a new dog did not transpire, for he and Rosie fast became friends. At night, they would find a way to get into the lounge and lie on the settee together. During the day, they would push themselves into James' room and stand on his bed to watch for the postman. Rosie had the sharpest bark he had ever heard and it always made the poor post man jump out of his skin. It made Spike chuckle. It was different to when Lady had been alive, for, whereas, she had been quite indifferent to everyone Rosie was really interested in everyone including Spike. At night time, they would talk together. Rosie was eager to understand the history of her new family and she listened intently as Spike filled her in with all the details. Rosie was also perturbed to hear about the grinning fox who had threatened Spike, she hated foxes with a vengeance. Sometimes, they would leave their trails of scent across the garden in the dark and Spike would watch Rosie's fur stand on end. The Yorkshire bloke would always let her out before he went to bed and Rosie would chase round the garden like a mad dog grunting like a pig. Spike was most amused by her. And then one night, Rosie shared her story with Spike.

She told Spike how she and her brother Ryan had been given away as two young puppies to an old man. At first, things were OK and they were loved and fed and fussed. But then the old man died and so they were taken away by a young man and woman who lived together. The house was dirty and messy and there was a terrible atmosphere of anxiety. They were both still young pups and not fully house trained but no one seemed to clean up after them or let them outside often enough to relieve themselves. As a result, they were often forced to sleep in their own mess.

On top of this, the young man had a terrible temper and he would shout at the woman and bang his fists on the wall. They were both very afraid in that house but the worst thing, Rosie went on to explain, was the terrible hunger for they were frequently left for days without food. Rosie recalled carefully how Ryan had tried to steal some meat off the kitchen side because they were so hungry. Even though they had both eaten it, Ryan got the blame. The young man caught hold of Ryan and tied him up outside in the freezing cold. He said it was to punish him for stealing. For two whole days, Rosie watched her brother freezing in the rain outside and she could do nothing about it but cry and whimper. Ryan would bark and bark and then someone knocked on the front door and Rosie heard an argument and raised voices, she was so frightened. She thought it was one of the neighbours complaining about Ryan barking all the time but then not long after that a man came into the garden and looked at Ryan and then he knocked on the door. He had a black uniform on and spoke very sternly to the man and the woman. And then he took Rosie and Ryan and put them in separate cages inside his white van. It was very scary as neither of them understood what was happening or where they were going. For two weeks, they had separate living quarters side by side, the floors were hard and cold but at least, they were fed every day.

"That's where we were separated," Rosie continued.

"Someone took Ryan and I ended up here. We never got chance to say goodbye and I still think about him. Sometimes when I'm on a walk, I run off for a while to see if I can find him. I'd know his scent anywhere but so far no luck. But one day, I'll see him I'm sure," she concluded.

Spike listened and thought how lucky he had been to find a good home straight away. He pondered as to whether Rosie's rocky start was in part responsible for her reckless side. For although she was tame and lovable, she also pulled some alarming stunts. On quite a few occasions, the blonde one would run into the house and announce to everyone,

"Rosie's gone missing on the farm."

Everyone would pull coats and boots on and help with the search; sometimes, it was hours before they found her or she reappeared. If this happened during the day, you could guarantee she had found a way into the fields where the sheep were. Spike watched her once from the top of the bank. The family had spread out in the opposite direction but Spike could hear the loud bleating of the sheep. He raced down the bank and sat on the dry stone wall surrounding the field of giddy sheep, this gave him a perfect view of Rosie chasing them in all directions. Eventually, the blonde one found her and ran into the field grabbing her and putting her on the lead.

The Yorkshire bloke had to help her lift Rosie back over the wall and out of the field. *It was most undignified*, Spike thought, but even though she was scolded, she would simply lie on the kitchen floor panting furiously to cool down. Spike knew she was delighted at the fun she had had, but he warned her not to do it again as the farmer might shoot her dead.

But she also went missing at night from time to time. She had found a hole in the garden hedge which gave her full access to The Roughs and all the night time smells and adventures. This would cause even more panic in the house. The Yorkshire bloke would be frantically searching and calling for her whilst the blonde one would drive around the streets.

"Why do you do it?" Spike enquired one night as she crashed out on the kitchen floor panting furiously.

"Chasing bloody foxes again," the Yorkshire bloke said as he followed her inside shaking his head.

Rosie winked at Spike. "You'll have no more trouble from that grinning vixen," she whispered.

Rosie could also be naughty inside the house, she had a similar obsession with food as Lady. This meant she would try to steal anything she could get her snout on, especially if it was left on the floor. Rosie excused herself due to the fact that she had been treated so badly as a puppy but Spike wasn't convinced. He could still remember Lady and her quest to eat the world despite her perfectly balanced upbringing. He resolved it was just part of being a dog, whereas cats were far more sophisticated. One night, Rosie learned her lesson good and proper though. It was Christmas night and eventually when everyone had retired to bed, Spike woke up to the sounds of chewing.

Rosie was helping herself to a large box of chocolate covered toffees which had been discarded underneath the Christmas tree. It was obviously an oversight by the family, as usually all food was kept off the floor in case such a robbery might occur. Rosie ate the whole box and then she started on another box of liquor chocolates close by.

It wasn't long before all this sugar and alcohol started to have a strange effect on Rosie. Spike laid himself out along the back of the settee and watched as she began to stagger around the room. Her tummy was gurgling and she was making some horrible smells. And then it began. Rosie vomited all over the settee and all over the rug. Then she waddled towards the conservatory and deposited another pool of sick on the smaller settee beside the blue chair. She was moaning and groaning and all her ginger fur was matted with the dark chocolate and toffee regurgitated from her stomach. Spike could only imagine the trouble she would be in in the morning especially as he had heard the blonde one complaining that the washing machine had broken down. As the sun began to rise, Spike decided to make himself scarce.

Everyone talked about that Boxing Day morning for weeks; in fact, it became legendary. But Spike and Rosie often chuckled about it together as they recalled the scene.

"You were a chocolate ginger nut!" Spike said, purring with superior satisfaction.

....

Spike and Rosie had spent the whole day inside due to the rain. Rosie was quite restless as she had missed running and walking and playing with sticks and balls. Spike was less bothered as he could choose whether to go outside or not and didn't care for the rain anyway. They had watched for the postman together but even he didn't appear. Rosie was bored and fed up. She tried to get Spike to play with her by jumping out in front of him. But Spike was not interested. The whole family seemed fed up as it had rained for days.

"Parts of the city are flooded," he heard the Yorkshire bloke announce later that day.

Rosie had eventually been taken on a walk but she looked like a drowned rat when she returned. She was also covered in mud and very smelly. Spike tried to spread himself out in her basket so she couldn't get in next to him but Rosie was undeterred. She stepped into the basket and pushed herself next to Spike's warm fur but the smell of wet dog was too much for Spike so he went to lie in front of the fire.

The rain was making it hard for everyone to get out and about and many roads were too deep with water to drive through. The blonde one arrived home late and had only just made it and all the family had tales of how bad their journeys home had been. Spike was just glad everyone was safe and he decided he would stay near to the house until the rains passed, for even he had not seen such bad weather before.

Eventually, the rain began to dry up and Rosie was beside herself with excitement. She was practically chasing her tail round and round in the kitchen as she watched Claire, the blonde one and the Yorkshire bloke all put their walking boots and coats on.

"Walkies Rosie, walkies," the Yorkshire bloke repeated, winding Rosie up more and more.

She loved it when they all went with her, it made the walk even more of an adventure and today, they had promised to take her for a long over-due extra-long walk. Spike watched as they disappeared through the garden gate.

Dan had left early to play golf and James had gone to town, so Spike wandered into the lounge for a peaceful sleep in the conservatory, it was then he saw Lizzie. She was on the phone to her mother and obviously upset. She put the phone down and sat in the blue chair. Spike wasted no time running across the conservatory floor and jumping onto her lap. Spike wondered what was wrong, Lizzie had been so much better recently.

"Meesha's died," she whispered to Spike.

Spike remembered Lizzie and Claire visiting Meesha at the stables, it was her mother's horse.

The news had been unexpected and now with everyone out, Spike knew he had to be with her. As her tears fell, they soaked his fur and Spike felt himself grow, he raised his body up and pushed his head into her cheeks.

Suddenly, everything that was familiar disappeared and both of them were standing in the middle of a town square. In the centre of the square was a small box office where several people were standing in line. Lizzie walked towards the line and joined the queue with Spike standing behind her. As people moved up the line and took their turn at the hatch of the box office, Spike could see that they were being handed whatever they were requesting. It was impossible to see what these things were but soon, it was Lizzie's turn.

"What's your choice?" the man in the office asked her.

"Err! Not sure," she said. "What do you recommend?" she asked.

"Well, most folk ask for heart shields and masks but not many pick the sword," he said.

"I will," she said decisively.

The man smiled and handed her a gleaming silver sword inside a holster that could be buckled around the waist. It was heavy and Lizzie struggled a little to lift it through the hatch and fasten it to her side. Once in place, she turned around and Spike could see it hanging from her side. It looked magnificent. Lizzie was the only one with a sword but, as the man had said, the others who had been in the queue were busy fixing masks in place over their faces or strapping large cast iron shields around their hearts.

Lizzie glanced around and then turned decisively to the left and headed along the street. Spike followed her and it seemed that she knew exactly where she was going. They followed the pavement until Lizzie found a door way which was painted black, it was the only door way on the street. She tried the handle but it was locked, Spike watched as she tried the handle several times but the door wouldn't budge. Eventually, Lizzie drew her sword and started to slash the outside of the door in order to gain entrance. It was hard work, but slowly, the wood gave way to the pressure of the steel blade making a hole big enough for Lizzie to push through. Spike followed her inside. It was dark and derelict inside and there was a smell of stale urine and cigarettes. Spike was alarmed to see how quickly Lizzie moved through the building, it was almost as if she had been here before many years ago. She held her sword up high and preceded to inspect every nook and cranny and open every door. There was no hint of fear as she moved from room to room. Every room was deserted and Spike wondered what she was looking for. Eventually, they came to a staircase which led down into the darkness, but

Lizzie never faltered, she ran all the way down with Spike trying to keep up. At the bottom of the stairs was a huge cellar, there were dim lights on the walls making it easier to see now and Spike could see a number of cages lined up against the wall. He instinctively knew that this was what she had been looking for. Lizzie stood in front of the cages and lifted her sword and Spike watched as she systematically smashed every bolt and lock off the cage doors. As she did, the cage door flew open releasing what Spike could only describe as animal shaped vapours. At first, they look angry and threatening but as they emerged from the cages, they instantly evaporated.

As Lizzie watched the last vapour disappear, a man appeared out of the darkness and stepped in front of her, he was also holding a sword. Spike growled softly and his fur grew stiff, but the man smiled at Lizzie. He raised his sword to salute her.

"One of us?" he asked.

"Yes," Lizzie replied.

"Well done," he said. "It takes courage to set yourself free."

As the conservatory came back into view, Lizzie sat for an hour stroking Spike. She was very still and calm and Spike knew the magic of the blue chair had penetrated deep into her heart.

....

As the other members of the family returned home, Lizzie broke the news about Meesha. Claire was particularly upset and the Yorkshire bloke was very quiet. Spike sensed how hard it was for him to lose both his dog and now the horse. These animals had been part of a previous life which had been taken from him. But Spike also knew that the Yorkshire bloke was not one to dwell too much in the past. As much as was behind him, there was much more in front of him. It was this strength that Spike admired and so he jumped onto his knee and as the Yorkshire bloke stroked him, he purred with steadfast zeal.

Chapter Thirteen

Breaking Through

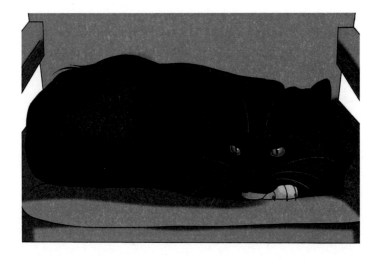

"Cats love to occupy your seat and feel where you have been

They love to steal your body heat and see what you have seen."

If there was one thing Spike had not discussed with Rosie, it was the magic of the blue chair. Somehow, he sensed that these adventures were very personal and that he was extremely privileged to witness them and be part of them. His purpose was to observe and protect his family and part of that was to keep all of these personal adventures as strictly confidential. He also surmised that as a dog, she would not be able to understand what was happening anyway. As Spike continued to reflect on what had happened to his family over the years, he felt he was beginning to see the effects of the blue chair and its magic.

For example, James had now moved out and started a course at university. He heard the Yorkshire bloke telling the blonde one how relieved he was to finally see James finish his 'gap' year of computer gaming. He was joking to some extent but Spike had heard many conversations during that year whereby the Yorkshire bloke had talked about putting a rocket under that 'Bloody Computer', as he called it.

One night, Spike was sleeping on the landing, he was laid out across Lizzie's pink fur on top of the chest of drawers, it was very late but even though everyone was fast asleep, he could still hear James tapping away on his computer downstairs in his room. Suddenly, the blonde one's bedroom door flew open and the Yorkshire bloke marched downstairs to James' room. His intention was to shout at James to get to bed and to pull the plug of the computer out of the socket. Spike was amused to see that despite the angry look on his face and the purposeful steps down the stairs by the time the Yorkshire bloke got outside James' bedroom, he simply knocked politely and asked if he could keep the noise down please. As he returned to the bedroom, Spike heard the blonde one say, as the door closed,

"Well! That told him."

But nevertheless, James had made it out of his bedroom, off his computer into the real world and whenever he came home, Spike could really see a difference. James was very much like his dad and he had even patched things up with his mother. There had been plenty of reminders from watching his step brother and sisters as to how fortunate he was to have both parents. It wasn't perfect as he thought it used to be, but it wasn't that bad either. Spike thought that university had brought the best out in him and he started to show his true personality again. He was very sociable and laid back and he never forced anything. Somehow as he 'let things be', life was working out for him. Although he was especially talented at losing things. Spike lost count of how many house keys the blonde one had to have cut for him and every time he left the house, she would constantly check if he had got his phone, his wallet and his keys. It made little difference though.

One weekend, James came home but he arrived early whilst everyone else was out. Spike was only aware of his visit when he began to hear some strange noises coming from the kitchen. Rosie started to bark and ran to investigate, but Spike followed more cautiously. The noise was due to a long thin branch being forced in and out of the cat flap from outside, Rosie pushed her head through the cat flap to see who it was, growling and barking. It was James. He had lost his keys and was trying to direct the branch up towards the back door key on the kitchen side next to the door. Now with Rosie wedged in the cat flap, he was giggling and stroking her head. Spike was trying to see as well but now Rosie's tail was wagging so hard it was bashing him in the face. Spike jumped onto the kitchen side knocking the key onto the floor with his paws. He could hear James' voice outside,

"Good girl Rosie, go back inside." He was trying to gently push Rosie's head back through the cat flap but she was so excited to see him, she was oblivious to the fact that she was in his way. James giggled again and tried to coax her out of the way but she wasn't moving. Spike had an idea, he noticed he had a few dry biscuits in his bowl which was on the kitchen side. Carefully, he slid the bowl to the edge and pushed it over. The sound caught Rosie's attention, she backed out and ate the biscuits in a flash as they spilled onto the floor. Now James could reach inside and recover the key from the floor to let himself in.

It was that weekend that Spike especially noticed how tall he had grown, but despite his manly stature, he could still giggle like a child. Everyone liked James and he settled increasingly into his new family, enjoying all the benefits that it brought to him.

There were other changes as well. Amy had spent quite a lot of time travelling and working abroad but now she too was off to university. Her heart was set on becoming a nurse and she especially wanted to work with people who were dying. Spike reflected on the young indifferent girl who had tried to avoid the pain of watching her own father come to terms with his death, and yet, she had grown into the most beautiful caring woman and Spike felt so proud of her. He thought her dad would be proud as well. Whenever she was home, she seemed to bring everyone together, it was like a gift. She got on with everyone. She had a great sense of humour which disarmed any potential stress or strife. She was quite a party girl as well.

The rest of the family might not always have seen this side of Amy, for it was usually seen in the early hours of the morning when Spike would be outside waiting for her to come home from a night out with her friends. Amy would skip down the pavement, trying to push her friends into the bushes of the next door neighbour's front garden. Sometimes, she would pick the flowers hanging from their hanging baskets and hold them in her teeth and then she would dance on the lawn in the moonlight. One time, she did a series of cartwheels down the middle of the road, her friends would giggle and she would shush them to be quiet. Her eyes would be big as saucers as she tried to put the key in the front door and then she and her friends would all stumble into the kitchen to drink tea and look at the photos they had taken on their night out.

To be fair though, Spike had seen quite a lot of this sort of night time behaviour in the other children. He couldn't quite work out why this behaviour only seemed to manifest itself at night except that sometimes when they walked home, it reminded him of how Rosie had staggered around the lounge on that Christmas night after eating the liquor chocolates. Dan came home late one night once and Spike ran to meet him. But as they walked down the road together, Dan decided to walk right over the top of the blond one's car parked on the street. He left big footprints and dented the bonnet. He claimed he had no recollection of doing such a thing in the morning but Spike had definitely seen him. Even James had done strange things. He had jumped out of a taxi one night and walked along the garden wall.

Spying his skateboard, he leapt onto it and rode it down the drive with his arms stretched wide like a super hero. He crashed into the dustbin and laid on the floor, giggling. Spike loved telling Rosie about it all.

These sorts of antics happened mainly at the weekends and Spike watched for the signs. There would be loud music playing in the bedrooms, hairdryers blowing, loud talking and laughter and then Spike would hear the sound of huge platform shoes clomping down the stairs. The scenes were quite theatrical.

Lizzie too would emerge from her bedroom on a Friday night with purple hair and black eyes. Her favourite pair of shoes were some green doc martins which she wore

143

with black leggings and layers of black and grey shirts or jumpers. During the week, she spent a lot of her time playing her bass guitar as she and a couple of friends had formed a punk band. Each weekend, they would play in the local pubs and no matter where or what time, the Yorkshire bloke was always happy to transport Lizzie and her pals to and from their gigs. Most of the performances were to raise money for animal charities or donkey sanctuaries for that was her passion. She had a real heart for the waif, the stray, the helpless and the abused and so the Yorkshire bloke wanted to support her as much as he could. However, Spike noticed he was never too keen to wait around and listen to their music.

Lizzie now had a large tattoo on her arm of a sword and a tiger. When Spike had first noticed it, he thought about the sword Lizzie had purposefully chosen during her encounter with the blue chair. He guessed she was setting herself free on that particular day, but now, she was using her sword to set others free. She had added two gold fish to her collection of unwanted pets as well as an extremely nervous Guinee pig that lived outside in the shed. All of them had tales of woe.

Increasingly, the atmosphere at home was changing. There were less arguments and tensions and new traditions were being established, Spike sensed they were finding their own identity as a blended family. More than once he had heard Claire say,

"But we always go to Cornwall for our summer holiday."

In truth, they had been twice and when it was suggested they go somewhere different, it was clear that Cornwall had lodged itself as a tradition in Claire's mind. It showed how quickly traditions can be established, especially when you are young. With that thought in mind, the blonde one and the Yorkshire bloke decided that they would create new patterns and traditions as much as possible, one of these new traditions was to go out for a meal every time one of them had a birthday. Rosie especially liked this tradition, as often, they would bring her back a doggy bag with bones in it. But Spike just loved the laughter and the story telling as they all came home. Sometimes, Spike would hear the blonde one reflecting on how expensive this tradition was but together with the Yorkshire bloke, they would conclude it was money well spent.

"We are investing in our family," she would say, and the Yorkshire bloke would nod his head in agreement.

The comings and goings still made for a hectic household though, but each of the family members were beginning to spend their energies on moving forward rather than raging about the past. The girls became sisters and the boys became friends and sibling rivalries began to disappear. Even Dan had a major breakthrough.

It was towards the end of summer. Dan had been much more settled in his work and was enjoying making money, driving and playing golf, and now, he had got himself a girlfriend. He had brought her home a couple of times and she had been invited to eat with them on a couple of family celebrations, everyone seemed to like her. But Spike had some reservations. They had been seeing each other for a few months and as with most things in Dan's life, he had thrown himself into the relationship with everything he had. There were never any half measures for Dan and consequently he was smitten.

He would take her out for meals, buy her expensive presents, and pretty much spend all of his spare time with her. But Spike observed a growing pattern within the relationship that he did not like. She seemed nice but Spike felt Dan was controlled by her. She didn't like it if he wanted to see his friends, so he stopped socialising as much. She didn't like it if he wanted to work out at the gym, so he cancelled his membership and she didn't like it if he wanted to play golf, so he even reduced that. Spike was more and more concerned. He was able to observe this growing trend in the relationship much more than the rest of the family because he could creep under Dan's bed and hear their conversations. It felt strange to him for he knew how much Dan hated to be controlled by anything or anyone. And yet here he was being controlled.

Spike knew there was a big golf tournament coming up at the beginning of September as Dan had shown him his entrance form and it was marked on his calendar with a big red circle. As the day came closer, Dan was determined to practice as much as possible. He was up at the driving range every evening after work and he tried to play a couple of games at the weekend. Consequently, his passion for golf and winning began to put considerable strain on his relationship with his girlfriend. One night when Spike was washing himself under Dan's bed, he heard Dan on the phone.

"Of course, I still love you but if I don't practice, I won't win," he explained, "if you've never played golf, it's hard for you to understand but yes, you still come first."

Spike could sense that Dan was increasingly out of his depth in this relationship and despite his best efforts, he did not seem to be successfully convincing her of his undying love, unless of course, he spent every waking hour with her. The more Dan wanted to practice, the more demanding she became, Dan was caught in a battle that he had not encountered before and Spike could feel his frustration and bewilderment over the whole affair. He spoke to his mum about it and the blonde one listened carefully.

"She sounds very insecure to me," she had said to Dan. "Just be careful you're not being manipulated, after all, everyone should have other things in their life that they love doing... I would have thought she should be supporting you and helping you."

Dan had not been sleeping very well at night either, which was most unusual for him, he would toss and turn and thump his pillow and even if Spike jumped onto his bed, he still didn't find any peace. Spike felt he was being pulled in two by the situation. As the tournament approached, the pressure grew but Dan dug his heels in and continued to practice. He was getting lots of support from the rest of the family but his girlfriend was nowhere to be seen.

On the day of the competition, Dan was up early and the blonde one was making his sandwiches in the kitchen. The Yorkshire bloke came downstairs to feed Rosie and Dan practiced his swing in the conservatory until it was time to go. He was usually told off for swinging the golf clubs inside the house but this morning, nobody said anything, it was a silent show of support.

"Good luck Dan," they called as he loaded his golf clubs into the car, even Claire came down to wave him off. He returned hours later holding a cup; he had won. Everyone was elated for him and the Yorkshire bloke set off to bring fish and chips back and buy bottles of beer and wine. Spike loved it when they had a fish supper and Rosie was beside herself. The whole family listened whilst he relayed his journey to victory. But still, his girlfriend made no appearance.

The next day, Dan slept late and when he got up everyone was out, he walked into the kitchen where Spike and Rosie were resting in the basket. He was staring at his phone. He walked straight into the conservatory and stood looking into the garden. Spike went to investigate. Dan was crying like a baby, the tears were coursing down his face and then he began to pace around sobbing. Spike was horrified at the change, for Dan had been so happy last night. Spike tried to rub up against him but Dan was pacing around so quickly that he couldn't get his attention. Quickly, he decided to try another tactic. He leapt onto the blue chair and began to paw it and meow loudly if only he could get Dan to sit down with him he might be able to help. The sound of Spike meowing incessantly eventually caught Dan's attention and he sat down in the chair with Spike on his lap.

"I've been dumped," he sobbed. The poor boy was reduced to a blubbering wreck but as Spike pushed his furry face into Dan's wet cheek, the magic of the blue chair was activated.

The familiar scene of the conservatory faded from view and they were transported to a long empty beach. Spike was sat amongst the sand dunes but he could see Dan standing closer to the sea, he was dressed in a wet suit holding a large surf board watching the enormous spectacular waves break. Spike looked out to sea and as he focused his eyes in the sunlight reflecting off the water, he began to make out in the distance the lone figure of a surfer riding the waves. He watched the surfer skilfully dance across the waves outwitting the surf over and over again, Dan was watching too, but he never moved. Eventually, the surfer rode a large wave onto the shore and began to walk towards Dan, it was a woman in her early forties. She smiled at Dan and asked,

"Are you coming in?"

"Not sure if I can do that," Dan answered.

"No problem, I'll teach you, it just takes practice… and a lot of courage," she laughed and beckoned to Dan to follow her into the sea.

Spike watched from the shoreline for what seemed like hours. Poor Dan, he was knocked down so many times but he never gave up, he would emerge from the surf with sand in his eyes and seaweed in his hair. The woman showed him how to wait for the wave and how to judge when to swim with the board and when to stand. Sometimes, he would stand up for a few minutes and then he would crash back down and disappear. The woman would fish him out and show him again. Dan listened to her and followed her and did everything she said and slowly, he started to get it. Spike watched Dan stand on the board and alongside the woman ride the biggest wave of all. It brought them both on to the shore. They were laughing and jumping up and down together celebrating their victory.

"You never know what the ocean is going to throw at you," she said to Dan, "but if you are willing to learn from others and keep going, you can learn to ride the very waves that have the potential to kill you, well done Dan."

Dan turned towards Spike and waved and as he did, the woman faded away and both of them were back in the conservatory. Dan stroked Spike and Rosie came across to lick him. He blew his nose and went back to his room.

That evening, the blonde one was sat in the lounge on her own, she was reading a book and Spike was sat with her. Suddenly, Dan appeared, he checked the room to see if they were alone and then he sat beside his mum.

"Mum, I'm so sorry for being such an awful son." The blonde one put her book down and looked at him. Dan continued, "I want you to know that all that jealousy and rubbish about you getting married again is in the past. Of course, you didn't want to be on your own, it's horrible being on your own and I didn't understand that until now. My relationship only lasted a few months but you and Dad had years together. I don't know how you've done all this and survived it and I've been no help at all."

The blonde one smiled at him and with tears in her eyes, they hugged each other but Dan still had more to say.

"And I've been horrible to Amy and Claire when I could have been a better brother helping them but I was jealous of how they just moved on, but that's over as well."

It was like a huge burden being lifted from his shoulders as he made his confession. The blonde one listened and nodded.

"Thank you Dan," she said, "but I have always believed in you, you're like your dad and he was a good man. I knew one day, you would remember who you were. But this has been really hard for all of us so don't be too hard on yourself."

Spike felt immensely privileged to witness this truce being made between son and mother and he knew that as a family, they had travelled a long way to this point in time. He also marvelled at the love and forgiveness but he knew that although the blonde one had not been expecting Dan to come and say all of this right now, she was also not surprised that it had eventually happened. Often, he had heard her speaking to the Yorkshire bloke about it.

"I know Dan will change," she had said, "I knew him as a little boy, he was so soft and loving, he has an exquisite heart underneath all of this anger and rage and I know he'll come through."

At times, the Yorkshire bloke had found it hard to believe but then the blonde one also found it hard to see beyond some of James and Lizzie's behaviour for the same reasons. And yet, the children were healing and growing as they yielded to the force of love around them; each of them were experiencing a breakthrough of some kind.

Spike jumped down and walked across to the blue chair, he jumped onto its soft cushion and began to wash himself. The magic of the chair was doing its work and deep down, he felt assured that all would be well, no matter how precarious it seemed at times.

Chapter Fourteen

Forming a Star

"Dear Spike, he is the king of cats, he's glossy and he's black

He commands your full attention and he's wonderfully fat."

Claire opened her eyes after a good night's sleep, she pulled back her covers and sat on the edge of her bed. Spike was stretched out on her rug but Claire was staring at Harry's cage.

"Harry didn't disturb me last night," she said to Spike.

Spike glanced up at the cage, the big book was still securely in place but she was right, there had been no noise from his wheel at all. She cautiously removed the book and opened the cage door. As she lifted Harry's bedding, the awful truth became clear… Harry was no more, he was stone cold and rigid. Spike was tempted to smile but it was Claire's loud sobbing that brought him to his senses.

"Mum, Mum," she wailed, "Harry's dead."

The blonde one came to console her youngest daughter who despite growing up into a young woman was still prone to be quite childlike and fragile. Claire was eventually persuaded to go to school despite her bereavement and the blonde one cleared the cage and popped Harry into an old biscuit tin that she had found, ready for his burial.

The house had slowly emptied out over the years and so the only children still living with the blonde one and the Yorkshire bloke were Dan and Claire. But even Dan was going to be moving out soon, he had got a new job selling for a security company and he was hoping to move to Manchester. He had certainly found his niche as a salesman and was earning good money. The blonde one often remarked to the Yorkshire bloke how much Dan was like his dad. She'd hear him making appointments on the phone and say, "When you're on the phone Dan, I close my eyes and it could just be your dad here in the room, he was a salesman as well, you know." Dan liked being compared to his dad.

Amy and James had both finished their university courses and had settled in the cities where they had studied: Amy in Bristol and James in Leeds. Spike had missed them coming home but realised they needed to make lives of their own and indeed, they had.

James had found a whole new circle of friends and a job and Amy was nursing and seeing a very nice male nurse called Mike who also lived in Bristol. Lizzie had moved to another part of the city sharing a house with two of her musician friends, but tonight, everyone was coming home. Spike had overheard the news that Mike had asked Amy to marry him and she had accepted. The blonde one was happily preparing the house for a full weekend of celebrations.

Everyone liked Mike and thought he and Amy made a great pair; Spike found him to be a very gentle, loving human being. Whenever he had met him, he would sit on his knee and purr until he dribbled, but Mike didn't mind.

The demise of Harry was, therefore, ill timed as this was bound to overshadow an otherwise happy occasion.

"Maybe we should bury Harry first before we all go out," the blonde one said to the Yorkshire bloke, "what do you think?"

"Will we have time though?" he questioned. "Don't forget Claire's not home until later as she's going to have her hair done."

"You're right," she replied. "I'd forgotten about that, OK, we'll just have to do it tomorrow, he's in a safe place anyway."

Spike and Rosie loved it when everyone came home, although Rosie made more of a fuss about it, she jumped and wagged her tail and licked everyone. Spike was far more self-controlled than that. The blonde one made a pot of tea for everyone whilst they waited for Claire to get back from the hairdressers and then they were all going out for dinner and champagne.

"I'm starving," announced Dan, "have we got any biscuits Mum?"

"Yes dear, I'll fetch the tin in," she said as she smiled to herself.

She was only a moment in the kitchen before she returned with an open tin in her hand. Dan reached inside with his eyes still on the TV but suddenly, he drew his hand back in horror. He grabbed the tin and looked inside, sure enough there was the dead body of a hamster looking up at him. For a moment, he couldn't take in the trick his own mother had played on him, but everyone was laughing hysterically.

"Don't tell Claire about this," she laughed, "but I couldn't resist to play a joke on the joker of the family."

Spike deduced that everyone had kept the little joke a secret; for the next day, Harry was laid to rest with suitable reverence and decorum.

Afterwards, the blonde one and the Yorkshire bloke took Rosie for her walk, leaving the children together in the conservatory. Mike had nipped to town so it was just the five of them. Spike had often noticed that whenever the children came home for holidays or special occasions, no matter how grown up they were getting, they would revert to a group of giddy teenagers. Today was no exception. Spike watched as Dan rolled up some old newspapers into a tight ball.

"Let's play dodge ball," he suggested.

Clearly, the newspaper was going to be the ball but it was Amy who announced that the blue chair was going to be the only place of safety.

It was a good job the blonde one was out, for the noise of raucous laughter was deafening and one of her pot plants nearly toppled over spilling soil onto the floor. It was good to see all of them having fun though, without any hint of anger or rivalry. All of the children had red faces and were out of breath and the ball of newspaper was getting more and more dilapidated leaving pieces of newspaper scattered all over the floor along with the soil. Spike had retreated to the settee in the lounge where he could watch the children playing from a safe distance. It was Dan's turn to throw; the girls squealed with delight and jumped onto the chair, then James ran across the conservatory in his socks skidding on the soil. The ball narrowly missed him but he made it to safety. The four of them were all hanging onto the blue chair, laughing and giggling then suddenly, Dan dropped the ball of newspaper and jumped onto the chair as well.

"Arrgh Dan, you'll break it," screamed Claire.

"You're squashing me James!" shouted Lizzie but they were all laughing.

Suddenly, Spike knew what he had to do, he jumped down from the settee and sprinted across the rug onto the conservatory floor and threw himself on top of the children.

"Spike!" they screamed, helpless with laughter. "Spike's coming too."

As Spike jumped onto the blue chair, the magic was activated and the familiar scene of the conservatory faded from view. The magic transported them into the carriage of a small plane that was flying high above the clouds. Spike watched as the children fixed their eyes upon a man dressed in a black all-in-one suit, he was also wearing a black helmet with a visor that covered his eyes and his nose. The door of the aircraft was open amplifying the noise of the engine as well as the wind outside. Each of the children were dressed like the man in black, except their suits and helmets were red. Spike could also see that they each carried a pack on their backs. It was this that gave him the sudden realisation that they were preparing to jump.

The man in black lifted his hand and showed the children his three fingers. Slowly, he mouthed the words three, two, one, dropping a finger with each number. When his final finger dropped, they disappeared through the door; Dan first then Amy, Lizzie next then James and finally Claire. The man in black watched the children falling for a few seconds and then, to Spike's alarm, he turned and grabbed him before jumping through the doorway himself. Spike could hardly breathe as they rushed towards the ground, he clung on for dear life fearing his fur might be blown off his back. The sensation reminded him of his first encounter with the magic of the blue chair when he had leapt from the high building. But that had been his decision in order to find his wings to fly. This time he had to totally trust the man in black. Suddenly, as his stomach lurched, he felt himself and the man being pulled back upwards as the parachute opened, allowing them to fall slowly towards the earth. Softly, they passed through the blanket of white clouds beneath them and Spike could see the patchwork of green fields and scattered houses below; he could also see the children. They were stretched out horizontally facing down towards the earth, their arms were wide and each of them had bent their knees so that their feet were pointing upwards behind them. But Spike could also see that, somehow, they had all managed to stay close enough to each other to hold hands in a circle. The formation looked amazing and Spike thought it resembled a red star shining in the sky. Suddenly, they broke away from each other and opened their parachutes in order to float effortlessly down to the ground.

Spike and the man in black were the last to land and although he felt the impact through his furry body, he knew that he was in safe hands. There was something strangely familiar about this man in black, something strong and secure. As he felt his paws touch the ground again, Spike ran towards the children. Slowly, the little plane came into land on the short runway in front of the grass where the children were sitting, they were all laughing and smiling. What a thrill they had all experienced together. The man in black walked over to them.

"Clever formation," he said, "you guys must have been practicing for ages to achieve that, I'm so proud of you all."

As he walked by, he reached out and squeezed Dan on his shoulder, Dan swung round but the man in black was nowhere to be seen.

Slowly, the scene changed and as the conservatory came back into view all of the children fell off the chair in a heap.

"Spike you were the last straw," Amy squealed and they all laughed.

Just then, Rosie returned from her walk and ran over to lick them all.

"Err! Rosie you smell and you're all wet, arrgh! Get off," they were saying, but Rosie was so excited to see them all on the floor that she just kept licking them.

The blonde one eventually calmed her down, wiping her paws and her ginger fur to help dry her off and Spike decided to escape upstairs where it was a lot quieter.

He trotted up the stairs and jumped onto the chest of drawers outside the bathroom on the landing. Lizzie's bright pink fur which was laid out on top was one of his favourite places to wash and settle down. As he licked his hind leg and his bottom, he thought about the blue chair and the magic which the children had experienced together. He felt this was highly symbolic of how far they had come. It was true, they had all practiced every day in one way or another in order to forgive and love and trust and become a blended family living and working together. The past had re-formed them and each of them, over the months and years, had practiced the skills required in order to overcome obstacles that seemed impossible at first glance. They had also learned how to absorb tensions and irritations which, if left unchecked, could have sabotaged their future together. But as Spike had seen from that perspective in the sky, when they put their minds to it and came together as one, their unity created a bright star-like image that stood out as an inspiration to others.

Spike nestled into the pink fur and thought about his journey of change too.

His purpose had been to observe and to protect his family through the lonely uncertain days of bereavement and grief. He had been chosen to help them grow and blossom and discover new ways of seeing themselves. But as he had accompanied them, he too had been transformed. He had learned how to live with those he had once mistrusted or hated or judged as his right to dominate or kill. He had shared his home with rats and learned to tolerate their lack of respect, he had resisted the urge to dispose of a hamster and allowed it to keep everyone awake at night and he had lived with two dogs, one of which he loved like a sister and slept with most nights. He had also opened his heart to the three new members of his family, helping them to heal and absorbing their pain as well. What a journey it had been, but together with the magic of the blue chair, they had reached a new place. *This is what it feels like to fly,* Spike thought, *this is what it feels like to be a king, it's when you know that you have a purpose and that you make a difference no matter how hard life is, or unexpected the journey.*

As Spike began to drift off to sleep, he could hear the whole family talking and eating together downstairs, it was a comforting sound. As he let himself fall into a deep sleep, he wondered how beautiful Amy might look on her wedding day.

....

Three weeks after the wedding day, Amy and Mike returned from their honeymoon. They had hired a big white van and they were loading it up with spare furniture and all kinds of bits and pieces that the blonde one said they could have. Spike was sat on the wall of the outside porch watching. He remembered how on the wedding day the Yorkshire bloke and Amy had stood in this very porch arm in arm. The photographer had taken several pictures of them before the Yorkshire bloke had escorted Amy to the black shiny car in order to give her away at the church. Since then, a big board had gone up in the front garden, 'For Sale' it read. More change was on its way. The blonde one and the Yorkshire bloke no longer needed a six bedroomed house and so the plan was to downsize.

"You nearly done?" called Mike to Amy from the front door. He was waiting to shut the van and head off back to their new home in Bristol.

"Yes just coming, Mum says I can take this and I think it will just fit on." She appeared with the blue cushion from the blue chair. "Can you fetch the rest of it please Mike?" she asked.

The final piece of furniture loaded onto the van was the blue chair. Spike watched and he wondered if the magic was still alive inside it. Mike and Amy petted Rosie and stroked Spike before they climbed inside the van and waved goodbye to the blonde one and the Yorkshire bloke.

"Love you both, see you soon," Amy called happily through the open van window as they all stood on the driveway.

Spike resolved that what was more important was that the magic of the blue chair was still alive inside each member of his family. He recalled the words of the man in the black boiler suit… "I'm so proud of you all." For this was exactly how Spike felt.

Rosie wagged her tail and rolled onto her back; she moved from side to side on the rough surface of the drive to scratch herself and Spike decided to join her; after all, there's nothing quite like a good scratch.

The End.